This book should be returned to any branch of the
Lancashire County Library on or before the date shown

The Jiggy McCue books can be read in any order, but to get the most out of them (Jiggy and Co are a wee bit older in each one) we suggest you read them in the following order:

Visit Michael Lawrence's website:
www.wordybug.com

And find loads of Jiggy fun at:
www.jiggymccue.co.uk

A JIGGY McCUE STORY

THE CURSE OF THE POLTERGOOSE

MICHAEL LAWRENCE

ORCHARD BOOKS

ORCHARD BOOKS
338 Euston Road, London NW1 3BH
Orchard Books Australia
Level 17/207 Kent Street, Sydney, NSW 2000

First published as *The Poltergoose* in 1999 by Orchard Books
This revised edition first published as *The Curse of the Poltergoose* in 2009

ISBN 978 1 40830 400 6

1 2 3 4 5 6 7 8 9 10

Printed in Great Britain

Orchard Books is a division of Hachette Children's Books,
an Hachette UK company.

www.hachette.co.uk

For
David Joby and Adrian Hayes
Old Playmates and School-friends
Good Kids

PROLOGUE

My name's Jiggy McCue and I have something to say about birthdays. They're rubbish. Mine are anyway. It's the presents mainly. When I was little I had terrific pressies – and so many more *of* them. Before I started in the Infants you couldn't move for presents on birthday mornings. Such great things too. All sorts of fascinating stuff. Even the bubblewrap was more interesting than the k.r.a.p. that's thrown at me these days.

My latest birthday, my twelfth, was the worst so far. I'd given the Golden Oldies a list of about 24 things I'd like (I try to help them out when I can) and guess how many of those I got. One. That's right, one. And what was that? A set of pencils. Yep. A set of pencils. And even they weren't right. I'd asked for 3Bs (to draw with) and they gave me an enormous packet of Hs, which I never use unless I'm forced to. I won't even *bother* to mention the other things they tossed my way. As

I opened them one after another I had to look happy and say, 'Hey, thanks, just what I wanted,' and hope I looked more sincere than I felt.

'I can take it back if it doesn't fit,' Mum said, holding a really drastic shirt against my chest. 'I kept the receipt.'

'Yeah, I see it,' I said, beaming like a melon quarter. 'Cheapskate.'

This wasn't me insulting my mother, tempting as it was. Cheapskate is the name of the shop she gets most of my gear from. Cheapskate sells everything, including kitchen sinks. Mum shops there because their stuff costs less than anywhere else. That's OK. I can accept that. My parents are always banging on about how poor they are. What isn't OK is that Cheapskate puts its name on all its products. This is just about acceptable on clothes labels, which are usually on the inside, but things like pencils don't have labels, so if I take them to school they'll roll around my desk with the word CHEAPSKATE in big glowing letters along each barrel, which won't do a whole lot for the cool McCue image.

My mother is the big organiser and shopper in our house, so Dad doesn't usually see the presents they give me till I open them, but let me tell you, an empty box would be better than some of that junk. Like, for instance, the Cheapskate shirt I got stuck with for turning twelve. It was my size — result! — but my mother's idea of shirts hasn't been in step with the times since I was eight. I'm either walking around looking like someone from the last century or I'm wearing a shirt with a big check pattern that makes me look like a trainee lumberjack.

Most of my birthdays fall on school days, and my twelfth was no exception. Fortunately, Mr Dakin didn't connect the dots and order the class to sing Happy Birthday, like he does when he knows one of us has one, so at least I was spared that. Pete and Angie gave me a cheap card (insulting, of course, and about as amusing as a hole in your shoe on a wet day) and said they'd be round after school with my present.

'Hey, really looking forward to that,' I said.

Angie looked at me suspiciously. 'Why do you say it like that?'

'OK, I'll try it another way.' I said it again, this time in falsetto. 'Better?'

'You know, I sometimes wonder why we're friends with you,' she said.

'Easy,' I replied. 'Cos no one else'll put up with your lousy hand-made excuses for presents.'

'Oh. Is that right. Well if that's how you feel, you needn't expect one this year. Come on, Pete. Let's go and mingle with people who *appreciate* us.'

'Who's that then?' he said.

She grabbed him by a bicep and marched him away. 'You really know how to kill a good exit line, don't you?' she snarled as they went.

Pete and Angie were supposed to come to the traditional birthday tea – just the three of us now I'm older – but Ange got her mum to ring and say they had sore throats and didn't want to infect me. So it was just me and the other human residents of our house at the table. Mum had made an effort, I have to give her that. But it was the same effort she'd been making since I was old enough to sit up without a support: crisps, sausage rolls, little jellies, and all the other things your average five-year-old expects on his birthday.

'Mum, I hate to tell you this,' I said, 'but I'm twelve now.'

'You'll always be my little boy,' she answered fondly.

'So when I'm sixty it'll still be butterfly cakes and balloons, will it?'

'It will if I have my way.'

'We don't have to play games afterwards, do we?' I asked nervously.

She showed her teeth, eager to please. 'Would you like to, darling?'

'If you do, I'm going to the pub,' Dad growled.

We didn't play games afterwards.

Mum had made a cake (squashed-looking, burnt at the edges) and put ten whole candles and one snapped in two on it. The candle deal was because she'd bought a Cheapskate B.O.G.O.F. (Buy One Get One Free) pack. The pack contained ten candles but what you got free wasn't another pack, it was one extra candle. That shop's not called Cheapskate for nothing.

All in all my twelfth birthday tea wasn't what you might call a memorable occasion, so I forgot about it immediately.

Afterwards, I went to my room — still wearing the phoney birthday smile that was threatening to splinter my jaw — and sank into the chair by my desk. I'd brought the Cheapskate pencils up with me because I felt I ought to look like I was keen to use them, and for something to do I started doodling with one of them (two would have been tricky). 'Some birthday,' I sighed. As I doodled, I thought back to the birthdays of my youth. The parties with bundles of neighbourhood kids, presents from everyone who came through the door, bouncy castles, games I actually *enjoyed*, candles that weren't broken in two to make up the numbers.

I hadn't really been paying attention to my doodle as I made it. It was just a pattern, nothing special. But when I did look I thought how much better it would've been with a 3B pencil, which is much softer and blacker than an H. Do I really have to keep using these till the day I put my mother in the Home for Really Senile Parents? I thought. I stuck my bottom lip out. 'No,' I said aloud. 'I don't.' I got up, dropped to my knees beside my bed, and hauled out the box I keep there for unwanted presents. I lifted the lid and threw the pencils in. If my mother ever asked where they were I'd tell her the truth. That they were in the Bad Presents Box under my bed.

The other things in the box only dated back a couple of years. This was because until I hit double figures most of my birthday presents were reasonably interesting and wanted. The stuff in the box included a stapler (still in its concrete transparent packaging), a set of screwdrivers, a belt, a Nicholas Cage DVD, a baseball cap (like I play *baseball*???), a plastic fly-killing gun, and a life insurance policy (yes, my parents gave me insurance on my own life as a present!).

Also in the box were some books I'd never felt the teensiest urge to read. Among them I noticed a school-type exercise book crammed with writing. The writing was mine, though for a sec I couldn't think what I'd written, or why. There was something sticking out of the book. The end of a white feather. The feather jogged my memory. Here was my account of the huge wad of bother I got into shortly after my eleventh birthday. I only wrote about it because Mr Hubbard, headteacher at Ranting Lane, said he'd have to suspend me if I didn't have a different story to tell than the one everyone believed.* Face-Ache Dakin read what I wrote too, and when he handed the book back to me he said:

'Useless as you are at just about everything, McCue, you have an imagination, I'll say that for you.'

'But it's true!' I protested. 'Every word!'

He did one of those laughs people do when they think you're spinning one, and strolled away.

I was about to close the book and shove it back in the Bad Presents Box when a few words on the page marked by the feather caught my eye.

The letters were luminous orange and as big as a house. My name just hung there, stretching from armpit to armpit like an axe murderer's grin.

This was a description of the stitching on the front of a hand-knitted eleventh birthday present from Bella Lugosi, my mother's mother. The very present that had landed me in the manure and got me the punishment of writing down what happened. The whole sorry saga came flooding back, wave after wave, in glorious hi-def sound

---

* It was being forced to write about that event that got me started on jotting down the other unbelievable things that have happened to me since.

and colour. I groaned at the memory, but now that I'd started, I had to read the rest. From the beginning. The utterly true story of…

Well, read it yourself. If you must.

WHAT HAPPENED

(The Truth)
by
Sir Jiggy McCue Esq.

CHAPTER ONE

My father had been out of work for years, on and off. He's always said it's because he knows his worth and won't take just anything. Mum says it's because he's useless. But then, finally, he gets a job that looks like it might last longer than a weekend, and to celebrate, he buys a new second-hand car to replace the fourteen-year-old heap we push round town instead of drive in. The new old car was sort of sky-blue with silver bits that hardly rattled at all, and you didn't have to kick little heaps of rust into the gutter every time you slammed the door, which was nice. We felt like royalty riding round in that car. Mum even looked a bit like one of the royals, but we didn't tell her, it would have depressed her for days.

The only trouble with the new car was that it looked all wrong on the curb outside our ancient terrace house. Some of the neighbours seemed to think so too, and when Dad had replaced the hub-caps and windscreen wipers for the third time, and sprayed over 'Rich sod' in a slightly different blue, he and Mum started talking about a new house to go with the car while it was still in one piece. So they got themselves a mortgage they couldn't afford and suddenly we were living on the Brook Farm Estate – in the house where all my troubles started.

The Brook Farm Estate is called the Brook Farm Estate because it's built on the place where Brook Farm used to be. Clever, eh? There's no sign of the farm now, it's all bright new boxes with half-finished gardens, but back when it was still a farm Pete Garrett and Angie Mint and I used to do odd jobs there during the summer holidays – collecting eggs, raking up cow muck, all the standard barmy farmy stuff. The farmer, Mr Brook, old Brooky, he didn't pay much and he wasn't that keen on kids, but we sort of liked going there because it was so open and all, and there weren't wheely bins and walls with bad wallpaper wherever you looked.

But then the miserable old devil spoiled everything. He retired. Sold the farm to a property developer and this new estate and shopping centre started to go up. When we moved in only about half the houses were built and the roads were still being laid and nothing much had been vandalised yet and it felt all wrong.

The new house was a palace compared to the old one, but I didn't like it at first. Didn't really want to like it. Pete and Angie came over quite often, but it wasn't like the old days when they just wandered through the gap in the fence when they felt like it. They thought the new place was cool. Envied me, they said.

'Yeah, but it's not like *home*, is it?' I said.

'That's what's so good about it,' said Ange.

We'd been in the new house about three weeks when Mum and Dad decided it should have a name. I wasn't keen. We'd always been able to find our house on Borderline Way without calling its name. I mentioned this.

'The house on Borderline Way was just the place we lived in,' Mum said. 'This one's different. It's special. It deserves a name.'

'I like the number,' I said. 'I think it's a terrific number.'

'What's so terrific about 23?' Dad said.

'I don't know, it just…has something.'

'We'll still keep the number,' Mum said. 'But a name will give the place an identity. Set it apart from all the others.'

'We've each put half a dozen suggestions in the hat,' Dad said. He shook his horrible *Help the Aged* bobble hat in my face. 'Thought we'd see what came up. Let fate decide.'

'Fate?' I cried. 'Fate? Have you any idea what fate can *do* to people?'

They just grinned, and suddenly I was very nervous. That hat could be stuffed with the kind of house names I'd never live down. I leant against something to stop my knees shaking. I think it was Stallone, our cat, because something scratched my behind and it wasn't me.

'Tell you what,' Mum said, 'to make it fair why don't you put some names in too?'

Now this was a surprise. 'You'd trust me to name our house?'

'Course we would,' Mum said. 'Wouldn't we, Mel?'

Blind panic stamped itself on Dad's face for a minute, but then he took a deep breath, cleared his throat, said, 'Course we would,' and reached for Mum's hand to give it a little squeeze. He'd been doing that a lot since we moved and it was starting to make me twitch.

'And whichever one comes out is the one we use?' I said. 'Even if it's my choice?'

'Of course!' they chortled like a pair of happy maniacs.

'All right then.' I reached for a pad and wrote down six names, right off the top of my head. They were going to regret this.

I folded my bits of paper and dropped them in the bobble hat. Dad shook them all up and Mum said: 'Who's going to choose?'

'It shouldn't be one of us,' I said. 'We don't want to get the blame.'

'Well there's no one else,' Dad said.

'There's no rush. Why don't we just wait till someone rings the new plastic doorbell? They can pick it out for us.'

There was a ring at the new plastic doorbell.

'Bingo!' Dad yelled.

It was Pete and Angie. I could have killed them. We told them about the house name deal and

23

they said cool and I said you're out of your minds, and they tossed for it to decide which of them was going to be the one to ruin my life. Pete won, and he gave me the evil eye as he stuck his mitt in the *Help the Aged* hat.

I suppose I shouldn't complain. At least the name that came out was one of mine. But when Pete read it out I said, 'No, no, do it again. That one was meant as a joke.'

'No, Jig,' Dad said. 'We made an agreement. Whatever came out of the hat was the one we'd use.' He smirked at Mum, who smirked back. '*The Dorks* it is then — agreed?'

CHAPTER TWO

Apart from the name it wasn't as bad at *The Dorks* as I thought it would be. For one thing the toilet flushed every time. That made a real change, believe me. And for the first time ever we had a built-in cooker which didn't blow all the fuses in the house whenever you boiled an egg. We had the same old junk furniture, but at least Dad and I could put our muddy feet up on that.

The most important room in the house of course was my bedroom. It wasn't like my comfortable old room at Borderline Way. It was neat, it was clean, tidy, even smelled nice, but I soon put that right. It was here, in my new room, that it all started.

The first thing that happened was Roger falling off his hook. Roger's my gorilla. I've had him since I was little when Dad brought him home one Christmas. He was drunk. (Dad, that is, not Roger. Roger doesn't drink, he's a toy). Roger has these very long thin arms and these palms which stick together when they touch. What you do is you loop his arms round something and join his hands so that he hangs from whatever it is. Like a big plastic hook.

Well there's Roger hanging from the big plastic hook on my wall and there's me sitting on my bed daydreaming about putting chewing gum on my most hated teacher's chair or something, and I must have been vaguely looking in Roger's direction because when his hands suddenly flew apart and he fell to the floor I jumped so high my head almost cracked the ceiling.

'You stupid gorilla!' I yelled, storming over. 'You almost gave me a heart attack!' Roger didn't reply. I picked him up. 'Nothing to say for yourself, eh?' I hammered his head against the wall a few times. 'One more trick like that and you're a rug!'

As I was fixing his hands together again — behind his back as a punishment — there was this crash. I spun round but I was too late to see it, so I could only guess what happened. My guess was this: my pillow, which I'd been leaning on a second before, had lifted off the bed, flown across the room, and slammed into my toy rocking-horse shelf.

I'll tell you about my toy rocking-horses. Mum had been collecting them for me since before I was born. She seemed to have got it into her head that I wanted the entire world supply of the things. I had about sixty by this time, all standing there facing the same way like an army of rocking-horse impressionists looking for a life, all sizes from so small they could fit in an eggcup to big enough to hold in two hands. Some of them were made of plastic, some of china, some of papier mâché, some of wood. Every birthday, every Christmas, every excuse, my collection was added to. Not only did I always know I was going to get another one (sometimes a whole family of them) but I could tell they were rocking-horses even before I unwrapped them. It wasn't difficult. Wrapping paper does not a disguise make, not for rocking-horses.

'Wow, thanks, Mum,' I'd say, all bright-eyed with surprise and gratitude. 'Thanks, Dad.'

'Don't thank me,' Dad would mutter. 'Last thing I'd give you is another bloody rocking-horse.'

This was the lifetime's collection of unwanted rocking-horses that my pillow flew at and scattered all by itself. All I could do was stand there gulping silently. My mother was just along the landing doing something with a duster. She heard the crash, stuck her head round the door just in time to stop silent gulping becoming a hobby.

'Jiggy, what on earth was...?' Then she saw. 'Oh!'

She came in, fell to her knees, stared about her at the Great Rocking-Horse Disaster.

'Oh Jiggy,' she said, and 'Oh Jiggy' and 'Oh, Jiggy, Jiggy, Jiggy,' until I finally remembered my name.

'Don't blame me,' were my first words after my hair stopped standing on end. 'It was my pillow, it just sort of...knocked them down.'

Mum glared up at me. 'Oh. I see. Your pillow. And you didn't happen to be swinging it round the room at the time, I suppose.'

Now this got to me. I mean I could see the way it looked, but I don't like being accused of things I haven't done.

'If you must know,' I said, 'I was over there banging Roger's head against the wall. If that makes the walls vibrate and sends pillows and rocking-horses flying, well all I can say is it's a pretty feeble excuse for a house we have here.'

'Oh look,' she said, obviously not hanging on every word, 'two of the most delicate ones are...' She reached for a couple of glass twins. Ex-glass twins. Now they were glass quads. 'These were my favourites,' she wailed. 'Jiggy, how could you, how *could* you?'

I felt myself go hot under the collar. What do you have to do to get through to some people?

'I'll say it again,' I said. 'I did not do this. Do you want subtitles for the hard of hearing? Do I have to get someone to stand at the side of the room speaking in sign language? Look. Read my lips. I – am – not – guilty!'

Bad move. The old girl went red in the face. Bug-eyed.

'Don't you *dare* talk to me like that, young man!'

But I was up and running now. Mouth open and flapping.

'I mean, yeah, right, sometimes I want to jump on rocking-horses till they rock no more. Some mornings I have this fierce desire to throw the whole lot out of the window and watch traffic drive over them till lunchtime. *But I am not the Brook Farm Rocking-Horse Killer!*'

Somewhere in all this a big change came over her. She went all sort of saggy and sad. Her forehead became one big crease and her mouth went down at the corners. Suddenly my 37-year-old mother was a hundred and five.

'I thought you liked them,' she said in this quiet little disappointed voice that grabs your heart and wrings it out like a wet sock. 'I really thought you liked them.'

Then she jumped up and ran out of the room with her knuckles in her mouth.

I felt bad. So bad I forgot to be miffed that she didn't believe me. It must have hurt, hearing my real feelings about the rocking-horses after all this time. I should have told her years ago. Got it all out of the way right off. My first words shouldn't have been 'Mum-mum, Dad-dad.' They should have been 'No lousy rocking-horses!' Then there'd have been none of this.

CHAPTER THREE

When I got home from school next day all the rocking-horses had disappeared. In their place was this bowl of white plastic flowers that a hand grenade couldn't destroy. That made me feel even worse. What had she done with the rocking-horses? I couldn't ask. And you know, I sort of missed them now they weren't there any more. I'd grown up with them after all, they'd rocked with me from the cradle, always been there whether I wanted them or not.

It was three days after the rocking-horse incident that the next thing happened.

I was in bed reading a horror story under the duvet by torchlight (the only way to read them) when suddenly…

Picture the scene. I'd just got to the bit where the two kids — Sam and Roddy — are pushing back the huge front door of this dark old house on the hill. They're there looking for their mysteriously missing friends and of course there's this storm going like the clappers – thunder, lightning, high winds, the works. Well Sam and Roddy push open the creaking door and there they are in this massive old dark old hall, which is very, very, very eerie. Suddenly the door slams behind them and the bolts are drawn across by this invisible hand, and there's this terrifying wailing sound, and then...

And then the duvet lifts off me, floats up to the ceiling, and winds itself round the Chinese paper lampshade.

'AAAAAARRRRRGGGH!' I said, or something quite like it.

While this was still bouncing round the walls collecting an echo, I heard Mum and Dad coming at the run from different directions, Dad taking the stairs four at a time, Mum shooting out of the bathroom. They were still on their way when the duvet yanked at the lampshade like it had a life of its own – yanked so hard there was a flash and the light came down, shade, bulb, the lot. I stared at the twitching, sparking wires in the ceiling and the burst duvet floating carpetward accompanied by a shower of white feathers. The duvet came to rest on the floor a split second before the Golden Oldies fell in, all wild-eyed and vocal.

Naturally, the first thing they did was flick the light switch up and down a few thousand times, *click-click, click-click, click-click,* before realising it was kaput. Silhouetted dramatically in the landing light, they took in the dangling wires. From the dangling wires they looked at me with the pillow in my teeth. Then back at the ceiling. Then back at me. A passing stranger would have thought they were into vertical tennis.

I jumped off the bed and ran to them. There are times in a kid's life when he has to make use of his parents or they might as well not be there. My head was already deep in Mum's chest before I realised it was not only wet but mostly nude as she'd just jumped out of the bath and pulled her dressing-gown on to get to me without delay. I shuddered, pushed both bits of wet chest away, and threw myself at Dad instead. And you know what he did? He pushed me away, held me at arm's length by the shoulders, saying heavy manful things like: 'Jiggy, what is all this?' and 'What have you been up to here?' and 'What happened to the light?' Questions, questions, when all I wanted was a decent hug and someone to say 'There, there, son, it's all right, you put your thumb in your mouth and I'll make you some hot chocolate and read you the Noddy book I've been saving for emergencies like this.'

Once I'd calmed down I explained what had happened, but I needn't have bothered. They thought I'd yanked the light down myself. And when they saw my horror novel they looked at one another, sighed knowingly, and confiscated it. Then they left, muttering stuff about not knowing what had got into me lately. And me? Did they give any thought to me? Did it so much as tiptoe across their tiny minds that I might be a bit upset about something? What do you think? I was left sitting there all alone on the side of the bed shaking and wet (part sweat, part Mum's chest), waiting for the duvet on the floor to move again. It didn't, and eventually I felt safe enough to crawl under the bed and attempt a spot of shut-eye, cuddling my slippers.

I didn't make it to dreamland. A sort of hiss jerked my eyelids back. I peered out from under the bed. The door was still open and the landing light was still on, which meant I could just make out the feathers from the duvet doing a little dance in mid-air. This time I didn't yell. I was all out of yell. I shot out from under the bed, threw myself across the room and along the landing, straight into Mum and Dad's room. Dad was just getting into his pyjamas and I gave him such a shock that he fell on the bed with his bare bott in the air.

'Dad! You've got to see this!'

'Oh, give it a *rest*, Jiggy!' he said, trying to sort himself out and recover his dignity.

'Go back to bed, darling,' Mum said. 'Enough's enough now.'

And that was it. I know them when they're in that sort of mood. Nothing will make them listen. So I gave up. Went downstairs. Spent the rest of the night scrunched up on the couch, shivering. I kept the light on. Didn't sleep a wink.

35

CHAPTER FOUR

I hadn't told Pete and Angie about the Great Rocking-Horse Massacre. I thought they might have a bit of a problem with it. 'Hey, you two, guess what happened to me last night, there I am sitting in my room minding my own business and my pillow throws itself at my rocking-horses, whaddayasay to *that*?' What they'd have said to that was 'Yeah Jig, fascinating, out of this world, come with us, they say the new doc down at the med centre's a whiz with raving lunatics.'

But now too much was happening to keep it all to myself. I had to share it with someone, and they were my best friends, so I told them – about the rocking-horses, the duvet snatching the light, the dancing feathers – and of course they covered their mouths and skewered their fingers at their heads, so I said 'OK, come to my house, I'll show you,' which wasn't very bright seeing as there didn't seem to be a pattern to any of this. I mean, like, why should something happen just because I'd organised seating arrangements?

Mum and Dad were both still out at work when we got to my place after school, but Pete and Angie rang their folks to let them know where they were. This was a one call operation. I should mention that although all three of us happen to be from one child families, Pete and Ange are also from one *parent* families these days. I won't go into what happened to her father and his mother or we'll be here all day, but the thing is that Pete and his dad Oliver had just moved in with Angie and her mum Audrey. To save on the gas bills, Oliver said. They must think we're stupid.

Up in my room we waited for the best part of an hour for something to happen. Then Pete said: 'I think you dreamed it.'

'If I'd dreamed it,' I snapped, 'Mum and Dad wouldn't have been so uptight, and I'd still have floor-to-ceiling rocking-horses and a light.'

Angie looked up at the naked wires. 'Is your dad going to fix that?'

'I doubt it,' I said. 'He doesn't like messing with

37

electricity. Doesn't even change bulbs if he can get someone else to do it.'

'So what happens exactly?' Pete said.

'Mum does it. Or I do.'

'No, I mean with this stuff flying about.'

I slapped my forehead. How many times did I have to go over this? 'How many times do I have to go over this?' I said.

'Yeah, well, it seems pretty funny that it only happens when there's nobody around but you.'

'I can't help that, I'm just the unhappy victim.'

'Hmm,' said Angie Mint.

We both looked at her. Her eyes were all screwed up and she was stroking the beard she didn't have.

'Hmm what?' I said.

'If you didn't dream it or imagine it, if it all really happened the way you say it did, it sounds like you've got yourself a poltergeist.'

Pete smirked. 'Poltergeist? As in ghost?'

'As in *mischievous* ghost. One that chucks things about and makes a general nuisance of itself.'

'Sounds like me according to my dad,' I said.

'There was this programme on telly about them the other night,' Angie said.

'I didn't see it,' said Pete.

'You were playing your Road Rage computer game.'

'What sort of things do they do?' I asked her.

'Oh, silly little things. Childish things, like...' She looked around for an example and fixed on the framed poster of some dolphins that Mum had hung above my bed because she likes dolphins. 'Like making pictures fall off walls.'

The picture fell off the wall.

I peered through the dust kicked up by four Musketeer heels galloping across the room and down the stairs. The front door was still rocking on its hinges as it became clear that this was only the beginning; that 'it' had just been waiting to get me alone, and now that we were...

For starters it whipped up the duvet and threw it over me so I had to fight to get out of it, which wasn't very easy. If you want to know the truth, it was like being held in the grip of a...well, a duvet. But when I was free I made a run for it, like Pete and Angie before me, though I didn't make it out of the house like they did. Furthest I got was the landing, then there was this hiss, followed by this

39

flapping sound, and next thing I know my legs are being attacked by something sharp and pointy and unfriendly. I ran into the bathroom, slammed the door behind me, turned the key. I was safe. Terrified, speechless, line dancing with the loofah — but safe.

Or so I thought.

SSSSSSSsssssssSSSSSSSSssssssss

It was in there with me! In the bathroom, jabbing at the toilet seat of all things, lifting it up, letting it fall, lifting it up, letting it — well, you get the idea. I reached behind me for the door key. My fingers didn't seem to want to work and the key dropped to the floor. I slithered down the door, fumbling about for the key. While I was doing this, the hissing flapping invisible thing found my dad's talcum powder. Talcum powder which, as usual, Dad hadn't closed properly to block off the little holes on top. And now, because of my father's *carelessness*, it was suddenly snowing talc that smelt of 'woodspice with extract of birchwood', whatever that is. In seconds the bathroom was covered in the stuff. So was I. I could hardly see for extract of birchwood, let alone woodspice. My only consolation was that I smelt gorgeous.

Half blind, half delirious, half wetting myself, I snatched up the key, found the keyhole, turned the key, flung back the door, and—

SSSSSSSsssssssSSSSSSSSsssssss

flap-flap-flap-flap-flap-flap-flap-flap

YYYAAAAAAAHHHHHHhhhhhhhhh

The last of these was me going down the banister one-handed, no feet, hissed at and flapped at and pecked at from behind. All this might have been easier to handle if I could have seen what was pecking on me, but I couldn't. Not then. I didn't get to see it till I made it to the living room. I'd just jumped on the couch and was about to plunge my head in one of Mum's big cushions, when the talcum powder snowstorm that had followed me in took on a shape.

The shape of a goose. A big goose. A big *angry* goose.

41

And then the talc was shooting off in all directions and the goose was trying to get at me through the cushion, and in a jiff the stuffing was on the outside and I'm standing there with an empty cover. I threw it away, dived under the coffee table — and discovered that it already had a resident, Stallone the cat, scared out of his fur by the thing that was after me. So there I was with my head under a coffee table while an invisible goose remodelled my back-end as a tea strainer and a demented cat tried to scratch my eyes out. Let me tell you, it was not a good position to be in.

Then, without warning, all this gratuitous violence stopped. The room went quiet, the goose stopped pecking me, and Stallone slipped away to do what he does best, which is lick like a madman between his hind legs.

My mother had come home.

She entered the room just as I was backing out of the coffee table. I saw her jaw hit the carpet as she took in a room that had not previously been covered in woodspice with extract of birchwood.

'Jiggy McCue!' she shrieked. 'What have you been doing *now*!?'

CHAPTER FIVE

My mother absolutely refused to believe that it wasn't me that had filled the house with talcum powder and shredded the cushion — not even when I told her I was being haunted by a goose. Her nose was still a bit in the air the following morning when she handed me the big soft parcel from her mother, my gran Bella. A belated birthday present. I gaped at it in disbelief.

Mum's eyes had a hard time staying in their sockets too.

'My birthday was ages ago.'

'Well, you know Bella. Even Christmas is a problem for her.' She read the note. 'It says here that even though she never sees you and she may not last much longer seeing as nobody cares about her, she wants you to know that she's thinking of you.' She looked at the sweater again, and flinched. 'You must write and…thank her.'

'Thank her?' I said. 'I'm thinking of sending her hate mail.'

She held the horrible thing against my chest. It was bright blue with my name on the front. The sweater, not the chest. The letters were luminous orange and as big as a house. My name just hung there, stretching from armpit to armpit like an axe murderer's grin.

When I went up to clean my teeth I kicked the late birthday sweater under my bed to fade quietly from living memory. Then I decided to have a stab at getting Dad on my side about the goose and talcum powder thing. You never know with Dad. Sometimes you can get through to him. Not often, because he doesn't usually listen, but sometimes.

He'd gone down the garden to look at his Rodadoodah bush. Our back garden is sort of L-shaped, and the bottom part is hidden from the house by a high fence. Dad's patch is round there, out of sight. He hates gardening more than anything except cleaning windows and cars, but he'd been going down there to check out the Rodadoodah on the hour ever since the big trip to the garden centre the Sunday before. They'd gone there to get things for this rockery Mum had been planning. She bought a lot of other stuff besides and planted most of it herself while Dad, worn out from driving ten minutes each way and carrying plants in, got a beer out of the fridge and read the paper. But she deliberately left a couple of things for him. 'It's your garden too, Mel,' she said. 'Perhaps you'd care to do something towards it...?' Which meant that he'd better if he knew what was good for him.

So Dad read the instructions tied to the leg of the Rodadoodah bush, dug a hole out of sight of the house, and dropped it in. But here's the thing: the following morning it was still alive! He couldn't believe it. Everything he'd ever planted had immediately committed suicide, and here was this Rodadoodah in bloom already. All right, it had been like that when they bought it, but that isn't the point. The point is that the dinky little pink flowers stuck all over it hadn't fallen off when he planted it and they hadn't fallen off the next day, and here they were, still in place three days later. It looked like all he had to do now was pray for rain occasionally.

'Hey Jig! Am I a gardener or am I a gardener?'

'You want to be careful,' I warned him. 'Get it right once and she'll have you out here all the time — even Saturday afternoons.'

I saw him go pale. Saturday afternoons were sacred to him. They were football-on-telly times, jump-about-on-the-couch-and-punch-the-air times. 'You might have something there,' he said, a frown dashing across his brow dribbling a ball of sweat.

'Don't worry. If it comes to it I'll sneak out one night and kill it for you.'

He looked relieved. 'Thanks, son.'

'Dad?' I said. 'What would you say if I said I was being haunted by a goose?'

'Is this a riddle?'

'No, straight question.'

'I'd probably say you're quackers.'

'That's ducks,' I said. 'This is a goose.'

'Oh,' he said, and his eyes glazed over. I'd lost him.

CHAPTER SIX

Before the Golden Oldies bundled me out of Borderline Way against my will, I always walked to school with Pete and Angie, but now that I lived on the Brook Farm Estate I had to go in a different direction, so our paths didn't cross. The way I went took me through the new shopping centre. That morning, like every morning, kids were swarming across the square, kicking tin cans about, yelling, cracking one another round the head with their bags, all the usual.

There were some men in the square putting up video cameras, four cameras, one on each side. There'd been so much vandalism in the shopping centre since it was finished six months earlier that it was already starting to look like it had been built by the Romans. There was this big campaign going on to catch the Brook Farm Vandals, as the local paper called them. Some people wanted them behind bars, others wanted them sent bungy-jumping without a bit of elastic. The cameras the men were putting up were big jobs, the kind you can't miss blindfolded on a dark night. Dad says they'd decided on cameras like that instead of neat little itty-bitty spy things tucked out of sight because no one in his right mind would vandalise things if he *knew* he was being watched.

I met Pete and Angie in our usual corner of the school playground and told them my news.

'A ghost *goose*?' Pete said. 'You're pulling my beak.'

'It's true, every word. Would I lie to you?'

He pulled open his sleeve and laughed down it. I sighed, and turned to Angie, expecting more of the same. But no, she was looking quite serious – and over her shoulder.

'I believe you,' she said. 'After yesterday I'd believe you if you said it was a ghost rhinoceros.'

'Angie, a picture got fed up of hanging around on a wall,' Pete said. 'Big deal.'

'Big enough to send you flying down the stairs head first,' I reminded him.

'I over-reacted.' He eyed Angie. 'We both did.'

But Angie wasn't having this. 'You were sick

with terror. You couldn't eat your tea, wouldn't talk to anyone, went to bed early with a hot water bottle even though it was a warm night. Mum and Oliver wondered if you were coming down with something.'

'What I was coming down with was common sense,' Pete said, all superior.

'Ha!' said Angie.

'You don't really believe all this stuff. You can't. Jiggy's putting us on, has to be.'

He looked as ruffled as a bad haircut. I don't think he expected Angie to take my side. All our lives we never went in for side-taking. We'd always been like that – you know, us against the world, one for all and all for lunch, and so on. But now that sides were coming up for grabs, Pete obviously thought Angie would be on his.

'If Jiggy says there's a ghost goose in his house,' Angie said, 'there's a ghost goose in his house.'

I tell you, if she hadn't been one of my best mates I'd have thrown my arms round her and kissed her.

'You must be going soft,' Pete said to her. 'Going all *girly* on us all of a sudden.'

49

Angie stiffened. Narrowed her eyes. She put her nose against his. Grabbed his shirt. 'What did you say?'

Pete knew he'd made a mistake. Angie has been a tough cookie from the day she gave up rusks.

'Just a figure of speech, Ange. Mind the shirt, huh?'

She put him down. I said to her (just her, Pete could do what he liked), I said: 'And I had the weirdest feeling coming to school, like I was being followed.'

'Don't tell me.' Pete's smirk was back in place, and it was awfully high on the Punch Me scale. 'By a dead goose.'

'Well yes, *actually*,' I replied.

'Heeeeey, is that the time?' He raised his wrist and looked at the watch he wasn't wearing. 'Gotta run. Urgent business in Sane Land.'

And he ran off across the playground to kick a ball about with a bunch of lowheads he would normally swim rivers to avoid.

'Don't mind him,' Angie said.

'What about you? How do I know you're not just setting me up for the big put-down?'

Ange looked offended. 'Jiggy McCue, how long have we known one another?'

'Since we were no-high,' I said.

'So do me the courtesy of believing me when I say I believe *you*, all right? Now. Tell me everything.'

I told her everything. About the duvet throwing itself over me, about being chased along the landing and down the stairs, about seeing a goose's outline in woodspice with extract of birchwood, about Mum thinking even *that* mess was down to me.

'And you think it followed you to school?'

'I might have imagined that. It might just be getting to me. I kept thinking I heard this sort of…hiss.'

'Hiss?'

'Geese do that. Remember old Brooky's goose? Chased us for miles just for setting foot in the yard once.'

Angie nodded. 'Scary old bird. Brooky called it his guard goose. Didn't need a dog with her around, he said.'

SSSSSSSsssssssSSSSSSSSSsssssss

We jumped three metres in the air, clutching at one another. '*Where did that come from*?!' Angie rasped as we came down.

Some of the nearest kids were looking at us. Bryan Ryan shouted over. 'McCue bothering you, Minty?'

'Get lost, Bry-Ry!' Angie shouted back.

'Yeah, get lost, Bry-Ry,' I repeated. Ryan shrugged and turned away.

Angie reached out and patted the air nervously. 'Can't feel anything.'

'You wouldn't, it's a ghost.'

'You said you felt it when it chased you. Your legs, your bum.'

'That's true.' I started patting the air too.

'Lookit them two,' Eejit Atkins said a little way off. 'Whacha doin', pr'tendin' t' be blind or sumfin'?'

'No,' I said, 'we're pretending to be stupid. We're doing Eejit Atkins impressions.'

'You wanna watch it, McCue. Less you wanna fump.'

And he walked off with his idiot buds, all rolling their shoulders, knuckles dragging the tarmac.

The bell rang. There was this startled noise close by, like flapping wings.

'What was that?' Angie said.

'The bell,' I said.

'No, the sound like flapping wings.'

'Wings flapping,' I said.

'What say we get outta here?'

'I say terrific,' I said as my feet hit the playground at speed.

Angie was at my side as we pushed through others less keen to get to class than us.

'Oi!'

'Watch 'oo yer pushin'!'

'Wossup wi' them two anyaah?'

And then there were other shouts, panicky sort of shouts, way behind us as we made it to the main building. The goose, the ghost goose, flapping and hissing its way through the crowd, was coming after us.

CHAPTER SEVEN

Face-Ache Dakin, our form tutor, isn't exactly what you'd call popular. He picks on you for nothing and is never happier than when he's handing out detentions and stuff. One of the kids who gets the worst treatment from him is his own son, Milo. I suppose he picks on Milo for the sake of it so as not to show favouritism, but on a good day Milo gives as good as he gets, which always goes down well with the class. He did even better than usual the morning Angie and I shook off the ghost goose in the playground. It was just after Registration, and we were getting our things out for one of Face-Ache's boring, boring, *boring* maths lessons.

'You, boy, stop talking,' growls Dakin.

'I wasn't talking, Dad,' replies Milo, then grins all round. 'Sorry, I mean *Sir.*'

'One hundred lines by tomorrow morning!'

'What for?' says Milo.

'For answering back.'

'Oh, I thought it was for lying – which I wasn't, as you know.'

'Careful, lad, or it'll be two hundred.'

'Sorry, can't do any lines tonight,' Milo says. 'Busy-busy.'

'What? What's that you say?'

'My turn for cooking and washing-up duty.' He turns to the class. 'Since my mum ran off with a jogger, we take things in turns.' He flips back to Daddy. 'Beans and chips OK tonight, Pop?'

'Stand up!' screams his doting father in this strangled voice.

'Right-o.' Milo gets up, hands in pockets.

'And take your hands out of your pockets!'

Milo takes his hands out of his pockets – and gets to work on his nose. I mean really gets to work. I don't know how he does it, probably a bit of string from his pocket, but he tugs this stuff out of one of his nostrils, tugs and tugs until it's about the length of his arm, like super snot. Even curls his tongue up to lick it as it goes by.

The class is having a hard time controlling its joy by this time, but his dad is not so happy. He storms up to Milo's desk and leans over him, neck out like

55

a spring. 'Young man, you will see me after school.'

He says this in such a way that you know, you just know, that he's forgotten for a minute that this kid is his own flesh and blood.

Milo hasn't. 'I will anyway,' he chirps. 'You're driving me home. As well as up the wall,' he adds, just loud enough for the whole class to catch. By now it's all we can do not to roll in the aisles with our legs in the air.

'Sit down! I will deal with you *later*!'

Milo sits. There's a halo over his head. His father returns to his desk and leans on it, fists clenched, glowering round at us, daring us to so much as titter behind our hands. He takes several deep slow breaths, then snaps suddenly to attention. 'I shall return in one minute! And I don't want to hear a sound in this room while I'm gone! Not a *murmur*, d'you hear me?'

He attacks the door, flings it back so hard it bounces, then slams it after him, rattling the roof. It's my guess he has to go and do some serious damage to the bike sheds, but whatever the reason, his absence gives the class time to collapse in grateful hysteria and give Milo a standing ovation and offers of money to teach us how to do that and get away with it.

It was while Face-Ache was away trying to keep his head from detonating that an even more memorable kind of hell broke loose.

It started with a hiss.

The first hiss was quieter than the noise of everyone getting out of their skulls, and Angie and I were the only ones to hear it, probably because we were half expecting it. Even Pete didn't hear it, though he sits right next to me. Not that he was sitting now – he was standing on his desk making rude signs at the door old Face-Ache had just gone through – but he sure felt it when he got beaked. Another word for that might be goosed, of course, which means that Pete got either beaked by a goose or goosed by a beak, depending how you look at it.

Anyway, he gave a yell and fell off his desk, and when he got up he was clutching his backside and glaring at me.

'Did you do that?'

I had no intention of answering this. Also, there were other things to think about than Pete's rear end. Like the shouts of terror from across the room

57

as six or seven kids started running round in circles followed by this great flapping noise as the invisible ghost goose chased them, hissing and pecking, pecking and hissing.

Fear spread through the class like wildfire. Before, there was just the cheerful noise of a roomful of kids celebrating the temporary departure of a teacher they didn't like. Now it was the panic of a roomful of kids being attacked by something big and angry that they couldn't see. I noticed that Pete's mouth had fallen open. It was trying to find words. It found two. They were: 'It's true!'

Now in an odd sort of way I felt responsible for all this. For some reason the ghost goose had decided to haunt me, and because it was haunting me it had followed me to school, and because it had followed me to school it was now attacking my classmates. Whether I wanted it or not it was my ghost and I couldn't just stand there and watch it go after the other kids.

I tore a curtain down from one of the windows. The curtain was orange, but that's probably not important. I stalked the empty space where the goose seemed to be. I tossed the curtain. It fell to the ground, empty. The goose had moved on. Now it was terrorising another batch of kids.

I changed direction too. Round and round the room I went, curtain held out before me, not even sure if you can capture a ghost with a curtain, even an orange one. Every time I thought I was close enough to run a test on this the goose swerved and left me with a curtain full of air. It wasn't hard to tell where it was because that was where things were flying around and kids were reeling and yelling and treading on one another's faces. There was hardly a desk left standing now. Our beloved classroom was rapidly losing popularity as a place to be. Kids were fighting one another to get out the door.

Somewhere in all this I heard Angie's voice. 'I'll go and find Face-Ache!' Then Pete's. 'I'll come with you!'

And suddenly the door was closed and the room was empty except for me. The ghost goose and I were alone.

Slowly, cautiously, I climbed over upended desks and chairs. The goose – still hissing and flapping invisibly, but less frantically now – moved ahead of me. It was over by the door now. I got closer and closer, curtain at the ready.

The door opened.

'Oh no you don't!' I cried, and leapt into action. I threw the curtain, then jumped after it, brought it crashing to the ground and put all my weight on it. It was moving under me but it wasn't getting away now. I'd done it! I'd got it! You *could* catch a ghost!

There was a muffled voice. A muffled angry voice. Not a goose's voice, which was a bit of a puzzle as it was coming from inside the curtain I was sitting on. It was saying something odd too. Something that sounded awfully like: 'McCue, I'm going to have your guts for garters for this!'

I got off the curtain. Looked under it. Face-Ache Dakin glared up at me with eyes like burning coals.

'Sir,' I said. 'Listen, I can explain everything...'

CHAPTER EIGHT

That night, while Dad hung about on the landing pretending he wasn't there, Mum sat me down quietly on my bed and told me that she was taking me to a behavioural psychologist. 'A behavioural psychologist,' she told me, 'is someone who tries to work out why a person does the things he does.'

I said: 'So why don't you take Dad to one?'

'Hey, don't bring me into this,' Dad said from the landing, blowing his cover without any trouble.

'Why would I take your father to a behavioural psychologist?'

'The way he carries on when he's watching football?'

'We don't need to take your father anywhere to know why he behaves like that. He behaves like that because he's never grown up.'

'Well neither have I,' I said. 'And I have an excuse.'

But there was nothing I could say. They'd

made up their minds. My parents were taking me to a shrink. They were going to have me shrink-wrapped.

Mum kept me off school the day of the appointment and we took the bus to town and walked to this old building full of offices where Serious People worked. The name on the door we ended up at had the name Dr Edward Pickett on it, with all these capital letters after it that didn't make any sense.

We'd been sitting in the waiting room for about fifteen minutes when this tall thin gent appeared, said 'Good morning!' in an unnaturally hearty voice, and held open his office door. I took the hint and went in. As the door closed behind me I knew that Mum was already reaching for the first *Hello!* magazine.

It wasn't a very interesting office. It had shelves with some fat books on, and a small neat desk over in one corner, and there were some filing cabinets and two red leather armchairs facing one another. The walls were covered with these big pointless paintings, all blobs and bits of colour that looked like they'd been slapped on with a mop or lobbed with a spoon. The kind of paintings I did when I was four.

The tall thin gent introduced himself as Dr Pickett (surprise, surprise) and pointed to one of the red leather armchairs. This chair was in the middle of the room, while the one he bagged for himself had its back to the wall, right under the biggest, most pointless painting of all. We both sat down and I tried not to stare at his hair, which believe me wasn't easy. The doc's hair seemed to end just above his ears, but on one side he had grown it so long that it would have touched his shoulder if he'd just let it fall naturally. Instead, he swept it up across his hairless roof, up and over, till it joined the other sad little batch cringing round the opposite ear. He must have oiled this long hair or something because it just lay there on top of his skull, glistening. I wanted to ask him a question. I wanted to say: 'Hey, Pickett, explain to me why an expert in the way people behave tries to con us he isn't as bald as a hard-boiled egg.' I didn't, of course.

'Make yourself comfortable, er…Jiggy,' he said, glancing at some notes on a small table beside his

63

chair. I made myself comfortable. 'Now I want you to understand that there's nothing to worry about here. We're just going to have a little chat about things. There's nothing to be concerned about.'

'I'm not concerned,' I said. I didn't tell him that I was more annoyed than anything. Annoyed that no one believed me when I said I didn't do things.

'For someone who's not concerned,' the doc said, 'you seem to be having some difficulty keeping still.'

'Oh, that's just me. I always jig about. Always have. That's why I'm called Jiggy.'

'Ah.'

He raised his hand to his face and spoke into it, so quietly I couldn't hear what he was saying. I felt I shouldn't be listening anyway. This was a personal conversation between him and his hand. While he was talking to his hand my eyes drifted to the picture over his head. It was one of those pictures you couldn't ignore if you wanted to. Pickett caught me looking at this and got kind of excited. It all began to make sense. He sat there under that picture and you sat opposite him, and every time you looked at it because you couldn't ignore it he told his hand about it, and later he played the hand back and decided there was definitely something wrong with you because you kept looking at this pointless picture all the time. This behavioural psycho game, easy money or what?

'Now, Jiggy,' he said, removing his hand from his mouth, 'I want you to tell me a bit about yourself. Let's start with school, shall we? What do you think about school?'

I didn't want to think anything about school. School and me didn't see eye to eye right now. Not since Face-Ache Dakin hauled me into the head's office for single-handedly destroying his classroom. Funny, but when it came to it nobody could remember being chased by something noisy, violent and invisible. All they could remember was me tearing a curtain down and going mad, jumping over desks and shouting and stuff. Even when Pete and Angie tried to come to my rescue it didn't do any good. Part of the reason for this was that they couldn't quite bring themselves to say that it wasn't me that had made all the mess in the classroom and terrified the kids, but a dead goose. You can see their point.

Dr Edward Pickett sat there smiling politely while I tried to decide what to tell him about school. The sunshine was sloping through the window really brightly and hitting the picture over his head so hard it glowed.

'What do I think about school...?' I said thoughtfully.

'In your own words,' said Pickett.

I was glad he said that. If he hadn't I might have rushed out into the street and asked a complete stranger what *he* thought of school and rushed right back with the news.

'It's...OK,' I said.

He leaned forward, obviously fascinated by my opinion on this subject. 'OK?'

I shrugged. 'Yeah. OK.'

'You don't mind school?'

I shrugged again. It looked like being a shruggy sort of conversation. 'Sometimes I can think of other places I'd rather be.'

'Such as?'

'Such as the bottom of a coal mine looking for canaries,' I said. 'Such as on the sole of a tramp's shoe when he's just walked in something a horse dropped. Such as at home, in bed.'

'So you don't think much of school?'

'I didn't say that. I said it was OK.'

'So you did.' He spoke briefly to his hand again. 'We might come back to school,' he says then, 'but let's move on now. Tell me about home. Your home life. For instance, how do you get on with your parents?'

I gave shrug three. 'We get on all right.'

'Just all right?'

'What do you want, violins and sunsets? They're my parents.'

'What I want, Jiggy,' Pickett said, like he was trying to talk his cat down from a tree, 'is for you to feel free to talk about them any way you please, in your own words.'

My own words again. I looked at his hair. Then, so as not to seem rude, I looked at the pointless picture above it. The sun coming through the window was getting brighter by the minute and the picture was so dazzling now that the colours looked as if they were moving. I was starting to hallucinate.

'My parents are great. Most of the time.'

67

I had to feed him that last bit. He needed it, I could tell. He had to have something to latch on to.

'Most of the time? Not...*all* the time then?'

'Do you get on with your parents all the time?' I asked him.

This threw him for a second. 'We're not talking about my parents, Jiggy.'

'Well look at it from my point of view,' I said. 'I mean we're sitting here across from one another, and you, who I never met in my life before, start asking me about my parents. I mean why should I tell you just because my mum brought me here? I'm not being difficult or anything, it's just that I think this should be a two-way sort of thing, that's all.'

He thought about this, then nodded. 'Fair comment. But there's nothing I can tell you, my parents are dead.'

I wished he had a big goldfish bowl so I could stick my head in it and drown. 'Hey,' I said, 'sorry to hear that. I didn't know or I wouldn't have asked. You miss them?'

'Miss them? Well yes. Of course. Sometimes. One does.'

'Does one?' I said.

'Certainly. One's parents, you know.'

'Did you get on with them?'

'We're here to talk about you, Jiggy.'

'All I'm asking is did you get on with your parents, like you're asking me, nothing heavy.'

He gave this some thought too. He was doing his best to be fair. Fair, or maybe he thought he'd get more out of me if he spilled a couple of beans too.

'As a matter of interest,' he said, avoiding my question, 'my mother painted the pictures in this room.'

I looked round the office. 'Yeah? Really?' Now he had me feeling sorry for him. 'Including the one behind you?' The sun was so bright on the big picture now it looked as if it was vibrating. A trick of the light, but it made me nervous.

Pickett glanced up, then back at me. 'That's my favourite.' He must have seen the pity on my face at that because his lips twitched in this way that says I know about these things and you obviously don't. 'I realise they may not be to everyone's taste. Art is such a personal thing.'

'You can say that again.' Fortunately he didn't bother.

'Now tell me about your relationship with your parents,' he said instead, with a very slight shove on the second 'your'.

'They'll do,' I said. 'I mean I wouldn't necessarily go to the Parent Shop and pick them out as the pair I most want to spend my childhood with, but they could be worse.'

Pickett flipped his hand to his mouth and while he told it about my parents I watched the sun leak out of the big picture and fan out across the top of his head. It was then that I noticed something. Something so attention-grabbing that I didn't hear a word of what he said to me next. I hadn't been imagining that the picture over his head was moving. It really was, all of it, not just the painting but the frame too. It was coming away from the wall. Falling. In a few seconds it would be off the wall and on Pickett.

And then, about three seconds after I realised the picture was going to squash Pickett, the sun cast a shadow across the painting.

The shadow of a long thin neck with a small

beaked head on top.

I jumped up. Ran across the space between the doc and me yelling something like 'Hey, watch out, watch out!'

I reached up, grabbed the picture by the frame, one hand on each side – but it was too heavy and I was too late! Even with me holding it, it continued on down, and there was this tearing sound, and next thing I knew I was standing there with the frame in my hands looking down at the top of Pickett's head, which was now poking up through the picture. He sat there staring up at me from the back of his dead mother's painting, his favourite pointless picture. The long strands of hair that he'd so carefully oiled on to his dome had come away. They were hanging down past his ear, past his jaw, his neck, the shiny brown ends trailing across the back of the canvas resting on his shoulders. And he looked terrified. Of me.

Then he was getting up out of his chair and stumbling about all over the place as he tried to wriggle out of the painting, and shouting stuff about me being a delinquent and a vandal and a hopeless case and a...

Need I go on?

CHAPTER NINE

The time had come to take my brain out of its box on top of the wardrobe, blow the dust off, and put it to work. I told Pete and Angie to bring their brain boxes too, and together we sat down on the floor in my room to think this thing out.

'Something's got to be done,' I said. 'Something has got to be *done*.'

'Yeah, but what?' said Pete.

'What we need,' said Angie, 'is to be logical about this.'

'Easy to say when you're talking about being haunted by a dead goose,' I chipped in. 'I mean there's logic and logic.'

'And dead geese and dead geese,' said Pete.

'And this,' said Angie, 'is no ordinary dead goose. It's a dead goose that breaks things and chases people and pecks them where it hurts. A poltergoose.'

I nodded. 'That's what we're talking about here,

isn't it? A poltergoose.'

'Right,' said Angie.

'Right,' said Pete.

'Question is,' I said, 'what are we gonna do about it?'

'Yeah,' said one of them, or perhaps both. 'That's the question.'

We put our brains back in the boxes. They hadn't worked.

Silence fell. And stayed fallen for some time until Pete suddenly said: 'Ow!' Then he said it again, with echoes – 'Ow-ow-ow-wow-wow-wow!' – and added 'Cramp!' He jumped up, but immediately fell again and lay writhing on the floor, one leg dancing in the air. 'Ow-ow-ow-wow-wow-wow!'

'I get that sometimes,' Angie said. 'Usually first thing in the morning, right after I wake up. It's *no* fun.'

'I don't think I ever had cramp,' I said.

'You're lucky.'

'Ow-ow-ow-wow-wow-wow!' said Pete.

'I get stitches though.'

'In your side?' Angie said.

'Yeah. And I don't have to be running or anything.'

'Know what you mean. I get them just trying to keep up with my mum in the street. Talk about painful.'

'Ow-ow-ow-wow-wow-wow!'

'And pins and needles,' I said. 'That's almost worse.'

Angie agreed. 'Right. Pins and needles. First time I had them we were visiting this sort of cousin of Mum's, and it was so...*boring* — know what I mean?'

'*Do* I?!' Old relatives. The things they talk about to one another. I mean what keeps them *awake*, that's what I want to know.'

'Ow-ow-ow-wow-wow-wow!' said Pete.

'This was one of those really brain-dead Christmas visits,' Angie went on, 'and there's this piano that the sort of cousin is playing songs from 1066 on, and there was nothing else to do but lean on it. The piano.'

'Tough,' I said.

'Owwwwwwwwwwww,' said Pete.

'And I'm leaning there and I get this weird feeling in my elbow that spreads through my whole arm, and I start dancing around yelling "I've broken my arm, I've broken my arm!"', and everybody laughs fit to burst, which didn't help at *all*. I mean *I* didn't know it wasn't fatal, did I? Adults!'

Pete stopped shaking his leg. 'Whew,' he said. 'Next time that happens I'm sawing it off.'

I got up. Walked across the room to put some music on. I was flipping through my CDs when Angie said: 'Oh very funny, Jig. I'm killing myself here.'

'Whassat?' I said, without turning round. 'I really must get some new stuff. There's nothing here under three weeks old.'

'How do you do that anyway?' Pete asked. 'Clever. 'Specially as we can't see your hands.'

'My hands?'

'You've been practising, haven't you?'

'What are you on about?' I turned round. 'Practising what?'

They were sitting there on the floor gazing at this stretch of wall that had been blank and would still be blank if it wasn't for the shadow on it. My saliva turned to dust.

'That's nothing to do with me,' I said.

Pete and Angie turned to look at me. 'You can't fool us.'

I watched the goose shadow's eye-hole close slowly, then open again. I held my hands out so they could see them. They looked from me back to the wall. The shadow was still there. The beak opened.

'You're...not doing that?' Angie said.

SSSSSSSssssssSSSSSSSSssssssss

She and Pete got up. Slowly. Backed away from the shadow wall. Slowly. When they reached me we stood as close together as we could without actually climbing into one another's clothes.

'What now?' one of us said.

'Run?' said another.

'Right,' said whoever's turn it was next.

We would have too. Except that as we set off at a fast tiptoe round the edge of the room, each trying to put someone else in front and someone else behind, the goose shadow turned its head to follow us.

But then the sun went behind a cloud and the goose faded to nothing. We gave a big gasp of relief. Three gasps. Angie stepped away from the rest of us to investigate the sudden shortage of goose shadow. And lived to regret it.

'YAAAAAAAAAAAAAAAAAAAAAH!' she said as she flew across the room.

Angie Mint lay in a crumpled heap on the floor just below the wall she'd almost hit. It could have been nasty. She might have gone just that bit further and ruined the wallpaper.

'You all right?' I said from where I was.

'Do you mind if I don't answer that?' the crumpled heap replied.

'Cool with me, Ange,' I said.

Angie came back across the carpet, on her end, a bit at a time like she was half expecting to be picked up and thrown again. When she made it back to us we stood waiting for something else to happen. Nothing did. Even the sun stayed behind its cloud.

'I think we ought to make a move,' Pete whispered.

'I just did and look what happened,' Angie said.

'Well I'm not sticking round here to be thrown at walls.'

'See you then,' I said.

'See you,' Pete replied. He didn't move.

'Well go on if you're going,' Angie said.

'I will, I will. When I'm ready.'

There was a long pause. Pete stayed put.

'When are you going to be ready?' I asked him.

'When I'm *ready* already, all right?'

'Right.'

An even longer pause. Then, very quietly, 'OK,' and he was off, heading for the door. Running.

But what a run. A run like no other I ever saw in real life. Not a fast-as-lightning get-me-outta-here type run. No, this was in slow-motion like in an action film, and there was nothing he could do about it. An unoccupied Zimmer frame could have passed him.

When Pete was halfway across the room, running for all he was worth at a hundred metres a month, the door opened. By itself. Pete looked happier about that than he did about running slowly. Door open, that meant he could go. He would be out there on the landing any day now.

And he would have been too if not for one small detail. The one small detail was that just as he was about half an arm short of it, the door closed again. The door closed but still Pete went on. He couldn't stop. He was going so fast now he could almost pass a wounded snail. He reached for the door handle. He turned it. Pulled at it. The door wouldn't budge.

SSSSSSSsssssssSSSSSSSSssssssss

Pete yelled, clutched the front of his jeans where he'd just been pecked, and bounced back into the room at suddenly normal speed.

Some minutes later, when we were once again sitting on the floor, backs to the wall, Angie said: 'You know what I think? I think the goose doesn't actually mean us any harm.'

Pete gaped at her in disbelief. 'Doesn't mean us any harm? After what it just did to me?'

'That didn't really hurt. It just gave you a little nip or you wouldn't have any colour in your cheeks.'

'You know,' I said, 'Ange might have something there. The goose could have slammed her against the wall but it dropped her short. And you know in class? It only *scared* the kids, nothing else. And when it pecked me down the stairs it didn't really do any damage, just sort of...rattled me.'

'That's right,' Angie said. 'I think it's simply trying to make us notice it.'

'It succeeded,' said Pete.

HONK!

Our heads hit the wall behind us.

'It's still here,' I said, in case nobody else had realised.

'And honking,' said Angie.

'Old Brooky's goose used to honk like that.'

'All geese do that,' Pete said.

'You don't think it could *be* old Brooky's goose?' This was Angie.

'Nah. Even geese have to be dead before they can haunt people.'

'Has anyone seen Brooky's goose about lately?'

'Well of course we haven't,' I said. 'The farm isn't here any more.'

'Probably lives with him in that new bungalow of his,' said Pete.

HONK!

'I think we'd better go and find out for sure,' said Angie.

HONK! HONK! HONK!

'Definitely,' I said.

We slid up the wall, very, very slowly. There was a low hiss from across the room.

'It's all right, goosey.' Angie waved her hands at nothing in a calming sort of way. 'We're on your side. We're the good guys.'

'We are?' Pete said. 'I thought we were trying to get rid of it.'

HONK! HONK! HONK! HONK! HONK!

We made a run for it. This time the goose didn't do any haunty sort of tricks like make us go in slow-mo, or open and close the door just as we got to it, or toss us across the room. Maybe it knew it had got through to us. Maybe we were on to something here. We threw ourselves down the stairs and out into the street.

CHAPTER TEN

The bungalow Linus Brook had bought with the dosh he got for his cruddy old farm was about where his cow sheds used to be. Like my brainless parents, Brooky had given his new home a name. The name he gave his bungalow was painted on a bit of black slate beside the plastic bell push.

LAST STAND

We pressed the plastic bell and waited till the national anthem finished so old Brooky could stop standing to attention on the other side of the glass door and open it.

'Hi, Mr Brook,' I said.

There were huge bags under his eyes and he hadn't shaved for a week. There was no collar on his shirt and not many buttons either. There was dirt beneath his nails, enough hair in his ears to thatch a poodle, and his teeth were yellow, black, or at the dentist's without him.

'Shove off,' he snarled. Same lovable old Brooky.

'It's us,' I said. 'Jiggy, Pete and Angie from Borderline Way.'

'Angie, Pete and Jiggy,' said Angie.

'Pete, Angie and him,' said Pete.

'Never 'eard of you,' said Brooky, and slammed the door.

We looked at one another. Something had gone wrong somewhere. Angie pressed the bell again. Ten minutes later when the national anthem had died once more, Brooky ripped the door back.

'You remember us,' Angie said brightly before he could get a word out. 'We used to help out on the farm in the holidays.'

'For peanuts,' Pete muttered. He never did care for old Brook.

'A lot of kids helped on the farm. If you can call it help. No reason to come bothering me here, I'm retired.'

He slammed the door. We stood looking at it, and at him standing behind the glass like a statue, either waiting for us to go or to try again.

'This is ridiculous,' I said.

'Yep,' said Angie.

'Leave it to me,' said Pete, and stepped forward. He didn't bother with the bell. He used his fist.

The door opened.

'I s'pose you think you can get a free cup of tea outta me,' Mr Brook said.

'Only if you're making some,' Angie said over Pete's shoulder.

'Making some what?'

'Er — tea?'

'Why would I make tea?' he growled. 'I hate tea. I always hated tea. Tea is my most hated thing on earth. After kids, that is.'

He slammed the door. Once again we stood looking at it. It was a nice enough door, but not so nice we wanted to spend our lives in front of it.

'Was he always like this?' I said.

'Like what?' said Pete.

I punched him on the shoulder. He punched me back. The door flew open. Old Brook grabbed us by the punched shoulders.

'Oi! I won't have you young layabouts fighting on my doorstep!' And he banged our heads

84

together. 'Now clear orf a'fore I buys a dog and sets it on you.'

While Pete and I staggered about groaning and holding our heads Angie stepped between us and put a foot in the door that old Brooky was about to slam for the fourth time. Being in pain, I wasn't paying much attention but when Ange said the word 'goose' I saw Brooky pass a hand over his eyes and his chest cave in.

'There used to be one round the farmhouse all the time,' Angie was saying. 'Remember her?'

Suddenly, Brooky let out this tremendous wail and fell face down on the Welcome mat, sobbing.

Angie dropped to her knees beside him. 'Mr Brook...?'

Old Brooky twisted his head from the neck to look up at her. His face was all wet.

'What a bird,' he said.

'Hey, that's our mate!' said Pete.

'I think he means the goose,' I said, still reeling a bit.

'Aunt Hetty,' said Brooky, and stuck his nose back in the mat. 'Sob, sob, sob. Sob, sob, sob, sob, sob, sob, sob!'

'Aunt Hetty,' Angie said over the sobs. 'Is that the name of your goose?'

'Was,' he said to the mat. 'Wa-a-a-a-a-a-as.'

'Was!' Angie sat back in triumph and beamed up at us. 'So she *is* dead! Good news!'

'EEEERRRRAAAAAGGGHHH!' wailed Linus Brook, miserable old farmer turned miserable old retired bungalow-dweller.

'Why don't we get him off the mat?' I suggested.

The pounding in our heads easing off at last, Pete and I got under Brooky's armpits and hauled him to his feet. Then we half carried, half dragged him into his living room. We were just about to drop him in a chair facing a cold radiator when Angie said: 'Look at this.'

She'd gone on ahead and was standing by the mantelpiece. We joined her, carting Brooky along with us. She was looking at a framed photo of the goose that had been better than a guard dog.

'Hetty.' Brooky reached between us and grabbed the goose photo. A great fat tear squeezed out of his eye, plopped on to the glass. He smeared it away with a thumb.

Then, bit by bit, we got the story.

Brooky told us that his wife had never cared for his favourite goose, Aunt Hetty, but when Mrs Brook died he took Hetty in, gave her the guest room. He called it the Guest Goose Room and decorated it specially, goosey wallpaper, goosey curtains, goose feather pillows, the works.

'Real company she was. Someone I could really talk to. Never could talk to the wife. All she ever did was sit there knitting and watching telly. But Hetty, she wasn't keen on the telly. Didn't seem to see any point in it. And as for knitting...'

'What happened to her?' Angie asked, all soft and dewy-eyed.

Brook was now sitting in a chair, the photo of the goose on his lap. 'I killed her,' he said.

Angie's face turned to stone. Her eyes went as hard as boiled sweets. Her voice became a foghorn.

'YOU KILLED HER? YOU KILLED YOUR *FRIEND*?'

Brooky shook so hard his last few teeth almost popped out. He shrank deep into his cardigan.

'I mean in a manner of *speaking*. I didn't *actually* kill her. Not personally. I wouldn't do a thing like that. If she was still alive I'd have her here with me at Last Stand. I...I *loved* that goose.'

Angie unclenched her fists and took several deep calming breaths and tried to look sympathetic again. 'So what happened?'

'I'd just sold the land,' Brooky answered, twitching in one damp eye. 'The builders were laying the foundations of the new houses and old Het didn't like all those strangers about the place with their thumping great vehicles, their radios, sandwiches and all. Thought they was trespassing. I had to keep her in when the builders were about.'

'*And*?' Angie said, just managing not to tap her foot.

'Well, my house was the last thing to go. They had to build this place for me before I'd let 'em knock the house down. But one day Hetty got out. I don't know how. I'd gone into town for my pension. When I got back she was lying there, squashed flat. Dead as a doornail. One of the builders had run over her with his bulldozer.'

'Goosedozer,' Pete muttered.

'They said it was an accident,' Mr Brook went on, 'and maybe it was, but I always had this suspicion that she had a go at them and they did her in. Saddest day of my life, that was, seeing poor Hetty lying there like that. No more honking, no more hissing, no more knocking the ornaments over when the national anthem started up.'

I leaned closer to him. I had a personal interest in this. 'What happened to the body, Mr Brook?'

'The body?' He looked up at me and gave another of his pathetic little sobs. 'It was all I could do to dig the grave. All my fault, see. That's what I meant. I as good as killed her when I sold the farm. If I hadn't sold up she'd still be here today, with me.'

'Yes. But where did you bury her?'

'Right where she fell,' he said. 'Right where she fell. I couldn't have carted her off to someplace else, I was too upset.'

'Yes,' I said. 'But where was *that*?'

'Where?' He gave this some serious thought. 'I don't know,' he said at last. 'One of the new gardens they was laying out, I think.'

'I don't suppose it's any good asking you...which garden?'

He shook his head. 'All looked the same to me. Still do.' He lifted the goose photo and stared at it, the tears welling up again. 'Felt bad about that later on, burying her just anywhere, but it was too late by then, the houses were sold. All private property and none of it mine.' He gave an enormous sigh. 'Should have given old Het a decent burial. The wife had one, and I liked Hetty better.'

When we left Brooky's there was one big question in our minds: if the poltergoose was Aunt Hetty's restless spirit and her body was buried in one of the new gardens and the garden happened to be mine, which *part* of the garden was she in? It would have helped quite a lot if Mr Brook had left a gravestone or something. Mum could always have grown something against it.

'Yeah, but even if we did find Hetty's body,' Pete said as we strolled back to my place, 'it wouldn't mean she's the poltergoose, would it? Necessarily.'

'Bit of a coincidence if she wasn't,' Angie said.

'Maybe. But if we found it and it *was* the poltergoose's...'

'Yes?' I said.

'Well, what would we do with it?'

'We'd move it. Bury it somewhere else. If she's somewhere else she might stop haunting me.'

'Then she might haunt someone else.'

'Their problem. Me, I'll be out celebrating.'

'Maybe Hetty's haunting you because she *wants* you to move her,' Angie said.

'What, to someone else's garden?'

'No, not someone else's garden. Perhaps she wants a decent burial, like old Brooky's wife.'

'I don't think they hold funeral services for dead geese,' I said.

'I don't mean an actual service. But from what Brooky said he treated her as almost human. So perhaps Aunt Hetty *thought* of herself as human. If she did, naturally she'd want to be laid to rest in a human sort of way.'

'You don't mean in a *coffin*?!' Pete said.

'No, I mean just...just something better than being dropped in a hole near where she hissed her last.'

'Like what?' I said. 'Like where?'

'If I was her,' Angie said, 'I'd want to be put in a place where I'd been happy. Like the farmhouse. I bet she loved it there. Yeah, bury her where the house used to be and her spirit might find peace and stop bugging people.'

91

'Snag,' Pete said.

'There's always a snag with you, isn't there?' I said to him. 'What now?'

'You know what they built where Brooky's house was?'

'What?'

'The new shopping centre.'

CHAPTER ELEVEN

Back home Mum was out in the garden working on her rockery. 'Nice rockery, Peg,' said Pete, the crawler.

Mum looked pleased. 'Well thanks, Pete.'

It really was coming on a treat though. She'd planted half the planet in it by this time and was as proud of it as Dad was of the Rodadoodah bush still being alive.

'Are you going to be out here long?' I asked her.

'Why, do you want company while you mow the grass for me?'

'No chance. Gardening's for wimps. Just asking.'

'As a matter of fact I'm going to the shops in a minute. Is there anything you want — apart from crisps, chocolate, fizzy drinks, and everything else that does you no good at all?'

'No, just those.'

We went up to my room. And——

SSSSSSSsssssssSSSSSSSSssssssss

The goose's shadow was waiting for us on the wall. Pete backed into me. 'Let's go,' he said.

'No,' Angie said. 'We have to get this sorted once and for all. For a start did you notice anything about that hiss? It was almost gentle. As if it's glad to see us.'

SSSSSSSsssssssSSSSSSSSssssssss

She was right. Gentle. Definitely gentle. Angie stepped further into the room.

'Goose,' she said boldly to the shadow on the wall. 'Goose, are you Aunt Hetty?'

And you know what the goose-shadow did? It winked. True as I stand here. Then dipped its neck a couple of times like it was saying 'You got it gal'.

'Yes!' I said, punching air.

'I have an idea.' Angie held her arm out so the sun cast a shadow of it on the wall, then opened her hand so its shadow was offering a palm to the goose-shadow.

And Aunt Hetty's shadow dipped its beak and touched the shadow of Angie's hand — very gently.

'Hey,' Pete said, impressed.

'You feel anything, Ange?' I said.

'Sort of a tickle. I think she wants to be friends.'

'Ask her if she's buried in my garden.'

'She might not like to think about where she's buried. She might throw me at the ceiling or something.'

'We've got to chance it.'

'You mean I have.' But she squared up to the goose-shadow and cleared her throat. 'Aunt Hetty, are you buried in Jiggy's garden?'

SSSSSSSsssssssSSSSSSSSsssssss

'Sounds like a yes,' said Pete.

'Ask her if she can show us where exactly,' I said.

'Hetty, can you show us exactly where you're buried?'

The goose-shadow nodded.

'Ask her if she'd like us to dig her up and bury her somewhere else,' I said.

'Would you like us to dig you up and bury you somewhere else?'

SSSSSSSsssssssSSSSSSSSssssssss

'Ask her if she wants to be buried where Mr Brook's old house was.'

Angie turned on me. She seemed peeved. 'Why am I doing all the asking? Your mouth seized up all of a sudden?'

'You're doing such a great job,' I told her.

'Huh!' But she asked. 'Hetty, do you want to be buried where the old farmhouse used to be?'

SSSSSSSsssssssSSSSSSSSSssssssss

'That is one clever dead goose,' I said admiringly.

'Not necessarily,' said Killjoy Pete. 'Maybe "SSSsssss" is the only word she can say.'

There was a sudden knock on the door. Have you noticed how knocks on the door are always sudden? Not only in books either.

'Can I come in, kids?'

Silent Panic. If Mum came in she'd see the...

We needn't have worried. The shadow of the goose vanished while we blinked.

I opened the door.

'I'm off now. Will you be all right here for half an hour?'

'Sure,' I said. 'Great. Take longer if you want. Take all day. In fact—'

'Thank you, Jiggy, half an hour should do it. I'm just getting a few things in for the house-warming dinner.'

'The what? Oh yeah, that. I thought it was tomorrow.'

'It is tomorrow, but I have some things to prepare and I want it to be really special.'

I glanced at Pete and Angie. They glanced back. All our faces said, Saaaaaaad. House-warming dinner. The things Golden Oldies get up to, breaks your heart.

The poor old parent was about to leave us in peace when she remembered something. 'Jig, I've been meaning to ask. Where did you put that sweater your gran sent you?'

'Sweater?'

'The one she went to such trouble to knit for you with her own hands? The one with your *name* on?'

'Oh that thing. I stuck it under the bed.'

'Well would you kindly *unstick* it and put it in your sweater drawer?' She turned away. I started to close the door. 'Oh, and Jig.'

Angie and Pete and I looked at the ceiling. '*Yes*, Mother?'

'Try not to turn the house to rubble while I'm gone – please?'

It wasn't till we heard the front door close that Aunt Hetty's shadow came back. Then I said: 'Ready, Musketeers?'

Pete and Angie nodded. So did Hetty.

'One for all and all for lunch,' three of us said. Hetty just hissed.

We went downstairs. On the way down we could see Hetty's shadow along with ours where patches of sunlight fell on the wall, but once we were out in the garden we couldn't see her at all. It was very bright out there.

'Aunt Hetty?' I said.

SSSSSSSsssssSSSSSSSSssssss

Which as everybody knows is Goose for
'Yep! Here!'

'Show us where you're buried, Het.'

There was a pause. A long pause.

'Perhaps she doesn't know,' said Pete.

'It may not be easy finding your own body,'
I pointed out.

'I never have any trouble,' he said.

HONK! HONK! HONK! HONK! HONK!

'I think she's found herself,' Angie said.

The excited honking had come from the far end of
the garden, the out of sight part of the L-shape. We
jumped over Mum's terrific new rockery, brushing
the flowers and stuff with our heels, and ran round
the corner. I was getting this sinking feeling.

'Say again, old goose,' Pete said. 'We're not
psychic.'

HONK!

The sinking feeling hit my trainers. My feet twitched. A Latin-American rhythm started to jerk through me. Dancing, I sniffed one of the perfect little pink flowers. Here of all places. Aunt Hetty's body was sitting right under the only thing my dad ever planted that lived. His pride and joy. The Rodadoodah bush.

CHAPTER TWELVE

After we laid the Rodadoodah bush on the grass beside its hole, we dug on with a spade and a couple of trowels from the shed. We all saw it at once. The sack that contained the body. We were pretty pleased with ourselves until we realised that none of us wanted to actually touch it.

'What say we cover it up again?'

'Mm. Good plan.'

'Could do it tomorrow.'

'Or the day after.'

'Even better.'

But like the good brave Musketeers we were we reached in and took hold of the sack, shuddered a bit, and tugged. It didn't want to come up, but we got it out eventually and stood wiping our hands on our jeans in case they'd touched worms or something else too disgusting to think about.

'Go on then,' Pete said. 'Open it.'

'No, you,' I said, breaking into a silent tap-dance on the turf.

'Your garden, your goose.'

'That's OK. Be my guest.'

'Oh – men!' Angie said, and elbowed us aside.

She untied the sack and spread it open. We looked in. It was not a pretty sight. Even Hetty sounded affected by it.

SSSSSSSssssssSSSSSSSSssssssss

Then the smell hit us. You could almost see it rising. Three earth-stained hands slapped over three noses, passing the stain on. Angie closed the sack.

'Better put the bush back,' I said, taking the lead in a fox-trot.

It wasn't till the Rodadoodah was back in it's hole that I stopped dancing and just sagged for a while. Without the sack down there below it the bush was about half its former height. (A couple of days later I found Dad walking round it, muttering 'I don't get it, I don't get it, I followed all the instructions. I even watered it once.'*)

---

* By then it wasn't just a dwarf Rodadoodah, it was a dead dwarf Rodadoodah without a single dinky little pink flower to its name.

Still, there was nothing we could do about it. 'Right,' I said. 'The shopping centre.'

Pete pulled a face. 'Are you out of your skull? Where was it your mother just went?'

'Oh yeah,' I said.

'Besides,' said Angie. 'Broad daylight when everything's still open might not be such a good idea. And we haven't decided where to rebury her yet.'

'I thought we said where the farmhouse used to be.'

'They built the main square over the farmhouse. We can't dig up the main square, someone might notice.'

'It's not all paved over. What we have to work out is where one of the rooms was, and if it's the sort of spot you can leave dead geese in we're in business.'

'Wait a minute,' Angie said. 'There's this big old tree in the square, with railings round it. Used to be in Brooky's front yard.'

'I don't remember a tree with railings in Brooky's front yard,' Pete said.

'It didn't have railings then, dummy,' said Ange.

103

'Yeah, that's right,' I said. 'The biggest branch hung right over the house. So all we have to do is see what's under the branch now. Good thinking, Angie.'

'What if it's solid concrete?' Pete said.

'Then we have a problem,' I said.

'Hetty's very quiet,' said Angie.

'Maybe something to do with the fact that she's dead?' said Pete.

'I mean poltergoose Hetty.'

'Probably in shock,' I said. 'Wouldn't you be if you came across your bones and stuff in an old sack?'

'Hetty?' Angie called softly. 'Aunt Hetty, you there?'

Not a sound. Nothing.

'Perhaps she's cleared off now we've found her body,' Pete said. 'Perhaps we can just chuck it over a hedge and go and watch telly.'

SSSSSSSssssssSSSSSSSssssss

'Or maybe not.'

There were several hours to kill before the shopping centre closed, so we had to hide the sack. There was only one place we could think of.

'Look, Hetty,' I said to the empty air, 'don't get your feathers in a twist or anything, we'll take you out later, I promise. It's just to keep you safe, all right?'

The good thing about the wheely bin was that it had been emptied that morning. It still whiffed a bit (though it was pretty sweet after the open sack) but it did the job. It must have been OK with Aunt Hetty anyway, because we didn't hear a peep out of her as we dropped the sack containing her sad old feathers and bones in the bin.

CHAPTER THIRTEEN

It was eight o'clock, the time we'd arranged to meet by the wheely bin. Pete and Angie were late. When they finally turned up Angie said it was because Pete kept finding other things he'd rather do than spend the evening with a dead goose. We flipped open the wheely.

'Holy underpants!'

'It's a conspiracy!'

'Unbelieeeeevable!'

Mum must have been saving all the household rubbish till the bin had been emptied, because it was now three-quarters full of used tins, sticky wrappers and old curry. All of it on top of the Hetty sack.

'We could always wheel it to the shops,' I suggested.

'People might wonder what three kids are doing pushing a wheely bin around,' Angie said. 'And we'd still have to get the sack out when we got there.'

'I'm not going in there,' Pete said. 'Here *or* at the shops.'

Angie called him a name I'd never heard before and took charge for the second time that day, or maybe the third. I raised an eyebrow at her. She was supposed to be the weaker sex. I'd have to have a word with her about this.

'Jig, go and fetch some rubber gloves from the kitchen.'

'Rubber gloves? There's only the washing-up gloves.'

'They'll do.'

'Can't. My mum's wearing them.'

'Terrific. Well I want *something* over my hands.' She mused. 'I know. Hankies.'

'Hankies?' said Pete and I together.

The boss snapped her fingers. 'Come on, come on.'

Pete and I fished out our hankies. Angie looked at them, curled her lip and shook her head.

'I'll risk the Black Death. Now tilt the bin. Tilt it over as far as you can.'

We tilted the bin until it was almost flat on the ground and most of the stuff inside had tumbled out. We pulled faces, grunted, said things like 'Eeeeerrrgg,' and then Ange — amazing Ange — reached in bare-handed, grabbed the sack, and pulled.

It didn't budge.

'You too,' she ordered.

'Not me,' Pete said.

She screwed her eyes up at him. 'Sorry? Didn't quite catch that.'

He took a corner of the sack in a finger and thumb. So did I.

'Get a *hold* of it!' Angie said fiercely.

We got a hold of it. A couple of hearty tugs and the sack was out and we sat there covered in bin droppings. Most of the garbage was loose stuff, easily shaken off, but the baked beans and curry and bits of soggy cereal seemed to get into everything, and I don't just mean clothes.

'You stink,' said Pete to me.

'It's my dad's new deodorant, *Wheely Bin For Men.*'

The next problem was getting all the rubbish back, which for some strange reason was even less fun than getting it out. When we'd done that we ran back shuddering to the garden for some clumps of grass to wipe ourselves down. (Which is how we came to have green stains all over us as well as the rest.) When we got back to the sack we found two cats sniffing at it with interest.

'Shoo!'

'Scat!'

'Get lost!'

Then, all set, we strolled off in the direction of the shops whistling different tunes, hoping that three kids pulling a sack looked normal. Most people ignored us, but a few grinned in that superior way grown-ups have when they're saying to one another: 'Kids, what will they think of next?'

Hey. If only they knew.

CHAPTER FOURTEEN

As expected, the shopping centre was deserted by the time we got there. (It's always deserted from about fifteen minutes after the shops close till about nine when the muggers climb out of bed and the drunks start rolling up to dance with the lampposts.) There wasn't even anyone snoozing in the flowerbeds yet. All just about perfect, in fact, for disposing of dead geese.

Until Pete spotted the downside. 'Major snag,' he said.

I sighed. 'What now?'

He pointed at the new security cameras. Angie and I groaned and the three of us stood with our sack of goose watching two of them panning for vandals. We would have watched all four, but a couple of them weren't moving. They'd been vandalised.

'There's the tree with the railings,' Angie said.

'Glad you pointed it out, Ange,' I said. 'Nearly missed it there.'

The big old tree that had once grown wild and free in Mr Brook's front yard now stood imprisoned in a neat little railing in the middle of the square. Everything else around the tree might have changed, but you couldn't mistake the enormous branch that used to hang over the house. It still hung there, over the place we had to put Hetty so she could R.I.P. and stop pestering me.

The Brook Farm Shopping Centre Public Toilets.

'The first person to say anything about feeling a bit flushed,' I said, 'is in big trouble.'

'Come on,' Angie said. 'Let's case the joint.'

'Hold on,' Pete said. 'One of the cameras is turning this way.'

We froze while the camera panned slowly by, then made a run for the toilets.

We waited while the camera panned the other way.

Then we ran back for the sack.

'Whew,' said Pete when we were at the toilets again.

I couldn't have expressed it better myself. This was nerve-wracking stuff. My feet had started moving in small rhythmic circles, my hips were swaying, fingers clicking.

'Will you stand still, McCue,' Angie said.

'Wish I could,' I replied.

There were two doors to the block of toilets beneath the branch. One of them had the word Ladies over it. The other had the word Ge ts, because someone had stolen the 'n'. The Ge ts was boarded up, probably because the graffiti-covered door on the other side of the boards hung on only one hinge.

'This one's OK,' Angie whispered from the next doorway.

We joined her, dragging the sack between us. There were no boards over this door, it hung on both hinges at once and hadn't been locked up for the day yet. Angie went in. The door closed behind her.

Pete and I looked at one another. Then we looked at the door. Then we looked at one another again. Then we looked at Angie, who'd just opened the door to look out at us.

'What are you waiting for, a personal invitation?'

'We can't go in there,' Pete said.

'It's only a toilet,' said Ange.

'It's a *Ladies* toilet,' I reminded her.

'So?'

'Well we're not ladies.'

'Camera's coming,' Pete said.

We pushed past Angie. The door closed behind us. Pete Garrett and Jiggy McCue were in the Brook Farm Shopping Centre Ladies Toilet!

'I'll never live this down,' said Pete.

'Nor will I,' I said.

'I won't tell if you don't,' he said.

'Deal,' I said. We shook hands, then wiped them on our jeans.

Then it hit us. And we thought dead goose in an old *sack* was bad?

'Phwah!' Pete said, palming his nose into his skull.

I agreed. 'No wonder there's a hole in the ozone layer.'

'Remind me to inspect the Ge ts sometime,' Angie muttered.

Pete and I looked around. We didn't like to, but it went with the job. What we saw on the walls shocked us to the core.

'I didn't know you got stuff like this in the

113

Ladies,' Pete marvelled. 'I thought it was only lads wrote this sort of thing.'

'The drawings aren't bad,' I said.

'When you two have stopped admiring the artwork,' Angie said, 'we have to decide where to put Hetty's bones.'

'No problem,' Pete said.

He kicked open one of the three cubicles and bowed like a magician expecting applause. He didn't get it.

'No,' I said. 'Not there. It'd be…disrespectful.'

'She's a goose,' Pete said. 'She'll probably think it's an honour to be flushed into the main drainage system.'

'You there, Hetty?' I asked through the filthy hanky over my face. 'How would you feel about floating out to sea, Het? You wouldn't be alone.'

If she was in there with us she was too choked with emotion to reply. Either that or she'd stayed outside because she couldn't stand the smell.

'We'd have to take her apart bone by bone to get her down there,' said Ange. 'And her beak would probably get stuck round the bend. We'll have to think of something else.'

'This is a public toilet,' Pete said. 'Public toilets have two things. They have wash-basins and they have...toilets. Got it, or am I going too fast? If you want to get rid of anything here that is the choice. Plug hole or bog. Do you want to take a vote on it?'

'There might be one other place,' I said, strolling over to the basins. There were three of them to match the cubicles. Below the middle one was the drain that all the gungy washing water slopped into. There was an iron grill over the drain. The grill had this nice flowery pattern on it. I tapped it with my foot.

'That's not much bigger than the toilet hole,' Pete said.

'It's big enough,' I said. 'We wouldn't have to pull her apart to get her down there, just get her to breathe in a bit.'

'See if you can get the cover off,' said Angie.

My eyes raced over the floor I'd have to kneel on to do that small thing. It wasn't all that clean but for the first time I was glad this was the Ladies rather than the Gets. In the Gets, the customers take aim at the wall, close their eyes, and spray everything they

115

can't see, including their feet, neighbouring trousers, and the ceiling. After a day's zipper action in the Gets, the floor is a swamp. At least this one was dry. I got down on it and inspected the drain cover.

'Anybody got a screwdriver?'

'Sure,' Pete said. 'I always carry a screwdriver. Would you like my hammer and nails while you're at it? My electric sander? My Black and Decker drill?'

Angie leaned down. 'What do you want a screwdriver for? No screws.'

'No, but I have to get something under the grill to pull it up, and a screwdriver would probably do it.'

'Use your fingers.'

'Use *your* fingers,' I said. 'Mine are reserved for earwax duty.'

She yanked me away from the drain, dropped to her knees and hooked her fingers into the grill. I watched, filled with admiration and disgust.

Pete wandered over to the door for a lung of fresh air. Angie and I were still crouched over the drain when I heard him say: 'What do you call a man in an envelope?'

'What are you talking about?' I said.

'It's a joke. What do you call a man in an envelope?'

'I don't know. Don't care.'

'Bill,' he said. No one laughed. Then he said: 'Someone's coming.'

'Is this another joke?'

'No. Someone's coming.'

'Who?'

'How would I know, she's not carrying a board with her name on it. But she looks like she's coming here — two guesses what for.'

There was a clang followed by a yelp as Angie jumped up and banged her head on the basin. She bolted past me into one of the cubicles and slammed the door. Pete bolted past me into another cubicle and slammed the door. I bolted past me into the third cubicle and slammed the door. This was the door I slapped my soles against after parking my jeans on the seat.

'Who's got the sack?' Angie's voice, muffled by distance and cubicle walls.

'Not me,' said Pete, also muffled but not quite as much.

117

'It's still out there,' I informed them.

There was a small pause. We could hear footsteps now, tappy-tap-tapping in the square.

'Maybe she'll miss it,' said Angie.

'Maybe she won't,' said Pete.

Another small pause. The tappy-taps were closing in.

Angie said: 'Something just occurred to me. There are three cubicles, and they're all full, two of them with boys.'

'Well?' I said.

'Well if that woman wants to use one she's going to be disappointed.'

'Good,' Pete said, 'then she'll shove off.'

'No, she won't. No one would use this place unless they were desperate. She'll cross her legs and wait for an empty cubicle.'

'She'll have a long wait.'

'We can't stay in here for ever.'

'Oh I don't know,' said Pete.

'Pete,' I said. 'Move over, I'm coming in.'

I separated my feet from the door, intending to make a fast switch to his cubicle and jostle for seat space, but just as I opened up the lady punter came in. I froze.

'Hi. Nice evening.'

She also froze. 'This is the Ladies,' she said.

'I know,' I said. 'I was just looking for something for my dad.'

'Your dad? In here?'

'Yes. He got the sack, then he lost it. Ah, there it is!'

I grabbed the Hetty sack and dragged it past the new customer, smiling hard.

CHAPTER FIFTEEN

Out in the square I hid behind the tree in the railings to fool the cameras. The seconds ticked by. I counted them into minutes. One minute, two minutes, three minutes, four. At the stroke of five and a quarter the woman came out and waltzed away. I lugged the Hetty sack back into the Ladies.

'It's all right, she's gone,' I said to the two closed cubicles.

'Whew!' said Angie.

Her door opened. So did Pete's. He peered out. All the colour had drained from his face. 'That was the worst experience of my life,' he said.

'I need help,' said Angie holding her hand up. It was wearing the drain cover. Her fingers were like knitting.

'Leave it to me, Ange,' I said, and bent her fingers back.

She screamed.

I bent them the other way.

She screamed again, but the cover was off.

We set to work.

It wasn't much easier forcing the sack of Hetty remains down that little drain than it had been getting it out of the Rodadoodah hole or the wheely bin, but we did it. That is, Angie did it, with me pushing at her shoulders and her telling me to stop. Pete watched the door. Every now and then he watched the square outside too. No one else came.

I felt quite sad when the sack was squashed tight into the drain and Angie had banged the grill back into place. I mean Hetty and I had been close in our way. I still had the dents in my backside to prove it. But we'd done it. Laid her to rest in the drain of her dreams. And I was a free man again.

When we left the shopping centre I strolled back to the sparkling new houses of the Brook Farm Estate, and Pete and Angie shunted off towards the Old Town and Borderline Way where half the street lights had been used for target practice and cars lived on bricks.

'Thanks, gang!' I shouted as we waved goodbye from a distance.

'It was a real pleasure!' Pete shouted back.

'Next time use a neighbour!'

Before I slipped out of the house earlier without telling Mum and Dad, I thought of leaving a compilation CD playing in my room, set on 'Repeat' so it would never finish and they'd think I was still up there. I didn't in the end because I decided that no one would be stupid enough to fall for that one. So the house was silent apart from the TV in the living room as I tiptoed upstairs and opened the door of my room.

Mum and Dad were sitting on the bed, waiting for me. My hand trembled on the doorknob. They looked a little tense.

'We were just going to call the police,' Dad said.

'The police?' I said, my recent life somersaulting past my eyes.

'Where have you been?' said Mum.

'To the toilet. I went to the toilet.'

'No you didn't. We looked in both toilets.'

'Hey,' I said, 'isn't it cool to be able to say that? Both toilets. Couldn't have said that in the old days, at good old Borderline Way.'

'I said where have you *been*, Jiggy?' Mum repeated.

'Why? Don't tell me I missed something.'

Dad chipped in. 'Cut the smart talk, Jig. Your mum's been worried half out of her tree. And you needn't say you've been with Pete and Angie because I phoned Oliver and he said they've been upstairs all evening playing the same boring record over and over.'

Mum leaned forward and spoke in italics. '*Where — have — you — been?*'

'I went for a walk,' I said. 'Round the estate. To see how the gardens are coming along, count the gnomes — you know.'

'Jiggy, I've told you before, I do not want you wandering the streets at night. The sort of people that hang round out there, it's simply not safe.'

'You've got to let me out sometime,' I said.

'Yes, well let's wait till you stop reading comics, shall we?'

'I still read comics,' Dad said.

Mum ground her teeth. 'Mel, that sort of remark doesn't help at all. Look at him, he's relaxed again.'

'Sorry, not much good at the heavy parent stuff.' He got up to leave. He was about to pass me when his nostrils shot out like a mad horse's. 'Ever heard

123

of baths, Jig? Or showers?'

When he'd gone Mum said 'Jiggy' in a much gentler voice and reached a hand out for me.

I took it, wondering if I should tell her to get a typhoid jab from the doc afterwards.

'Yes, Mum?'

She pulled me closer. Her nostrils flared too but she was too much of a gentleman to shudder. She sat me down beside her.

'Jiggy,' she said again.

'Still here,' I said.

'Promise me you won't do anything like that again.'

'What, go out? You mean not even to school? Can I have that in writing?'

'You know what I'm talking about.' Her eyes went all big and soft, and she added: 'You're all we've got, you know.'

'Well that's not quite true,' I said. 'You've got the car, the TV, the washing machine, your curling tongs. And don't forget Stallone.'

She threw my hand away, probably realising it was contaminated, and stood up. She seemed upset about something.

'There's no point even *trying* to talk to you, is there? Well pay attention to this. I want you out of those things right this minute. You will then go and have a good wash – and I mean good wash – and go straight to bed. I don't want to see hide nor hair of you till tomorrow morning, when I expect a full apology for worrying me sick. Do I make myself clear?'

'Yes, Mum.'

She went. I leaned back on the bed. Suddenly I felt tired. Very, *very* tired. All I wanted was to get in there under the duvet and not wake up till the end of the week when school was over. Still, I had the satisfaction of knowing that my poltergoose troubles were over. Never again would I see Aunt Hetty's shadow on my wall. Never again see rocking-horses butchered before my eyes or gorillas fall off hooks or lights torn from ceilings. Never again would I be chased downstairs by a beak.

There was probably a happy grin on my face as my bed suddenly tipped up, flew across the room, and hit the opposite wall with me still on it. As the bed rocked back on its castors and I rolled on to the floor with the bowl of white plastic flowers in my hands, an insane honking, like no honking I ever heard before, filled the room. Then my mother and father were rushing in again screaming my name and threatening to ground me for the rest of my life if I didn't stop this outrageous, this childish, this totally unacceptable behaviour.

Home, sweet home.

CHAPTER SIXTEEN

So Hetty didn't care for life after death in a public drain and she wasn't going to leave me in peace till we found her some place more to her liking.

'Pity she didn't mention it before,' Angie said when I told her and Pete at school next day.

'And where else are we supposed to put her?' Pete said.

'I don't know, but it has to be soon, like tonight. At breakfast my dad was looking through *Yellow Pages* for junior straitjacket suppliers.'

'We can't do anything tonight. Your parents' house-warming dinner thing.'

'If we don't do it tonight,' I said, 'Hetty might lose her goosey cool and completely destroy the house-warming dinner thing, along with what's left of my sanity.'

'Jiggy's right,' said Angie. 'We have to act fast.'

We arranged to meet by the shopping centre at eight to haul Hetty out of the Ladies and back to my place. The plan was to stick her under the dwarf Rodadoodah again till we figured out what to do next. But then, just before tea, Angie phoned and told me to bring a spade.

'What do we want a spade for?' I asked. 'We can pull her out.'

'It's for putting her where she ought to be.'

'We don't know where she ought to be.'

'I do,' she said. 'I went back to the shopping centre after school and realised where we went wrong. Tell you later. Eight o'clock, with spade.'

At ten to eight, all dressed up in the clothes my mother laid out specially to make me feel really stupid (creases down the front of my jeans and all) I stuck my head round the kitchen door. Mum was bending over the stove like a witch, stirring something, and Dad was sitting on a stool looking at the pictures in the free local paper he never reads.

'Mum, what time's this dinner thing?'

'I told Aud and Ollie eight for eight-thirty.'

'What does that mean?'

'Means we sit down to eat on the dot of 9.43,' Dad muttered from behind the paper.

'So I've got…how long exactly?'

'One hour,' said Mum.

'And a half,' said Dad. 'At least.'

'Where do you think you're going anyway?' Mum asked.

'Meeting Pete and Ange. We'll have a little chat, then they'll come back with me.'

'In that case you can go upstairs and put a jumper on. I don't want you getting that clean shirt dirty.'

'I won't get it dirty.'

'Don't argue or I'll remember what I said last night about you not going out again as long as you live.'

I tore all my hair out, jumped on it, ran back up to my room, grabbed the first woolly thing in my sweater drawer, stuck my head through it, and hopped down again six stairs at a time.

Out in the garden I whipped a spade from the shed. Then I legged it for the shopping centre. Like last time, the square was deserted and quiet. Angie and Pete were already there, standing well back from the cameras. Like me, they were in their best togs with embarrassing creases down the front of their jeans.

The first thing Angie said when I jogged into view wasn't, as you might expect, 'Hi, Jig, glad you could make it, see you got the spade, you're my hero.' No, it was: 'Jiggy McCue, are you out of your pathetic excuse for a *mind*?'

'Naturally, only place to be,' I zapped back. 'Why do you ask?'

'The sweater?' she said wearily.

I looked down at my sweater from on high. It was the one Bella, my gran, had knitted with her own wrinkly little hands. The blue one with JIGGY screaming across the front in luminous orange letters as big as an elephant's behind. My mother had asked me to remove it from under my bed and when I didn't she must have rescued it and put it in my sweater drawer on top of everything else.

I heard a small gasping sound near my feet. Pete's knees had given way and he was folded up on the ground in silent hysterics. Angie and I stood looking at the sky while he gagged down there for another minute, then he got up, tears streaming down his neck. He couldn't look at me without starting again.

The Ladies toilet sat across the square, waiting for us. 'Anyone in there?' I asked Angie.

'Not unless they've got a problem. We've been here ten minutes. Come on, and mind those cameras.'

We loaded our feet and fired them across the square. It wasn't till we reached the Ladies and were halfway through the door that we noticed dirty water splashing up our nice clean jeans. This took our attention away from the smell of the place, but we may have forgotten to be grateful as we slithered to a halt at the wash-basins. The water was bubbling up from the drain underneath instead of gurgling gently into it.

'Must be blocked up with something,' Pete said, wading back to the door.

'I'm not putting my hand down there this time,' Angie said.

'Come on, Ange,' I said. 'You're so good at it.'

'Well it's about time someone *else* got good at it then, isn't it? Like you.'

'But I'll get all wet,' I said. 'Wetter.'

'Get down there, McCue. Now!'

She was in that dangerous mood again. I rolled up my hand-knitted sleeves, plunged a neatly

131

creased knee into the canal that swirled about us, and closed my eyes in misery.

'What's it feel like?' Pete said, leaning in the door on his toes.

'Shut up,' I said.

The drain cover was all slimy, like seaweed or poached slugs. My stomach turned over as I stuck my fingers through its fancy holes. I tugged. The grill didn't budge. I tugged again. Slight movement. I put everything I had into it – and shot backwards, full length, into the water, fingers neatly interwoven with the pretty iron pattern.

'You wanna be careful,' Pete said from the door. 'Spoil your nice party clothes.'

'Angie,' I said, splashing to my feet, 'untie my fingers, will you? I want to put them in Pete's eyes.'

'Get away from me,' she said. 'I'm as wet I'm going to get.'

'*You're* wet?' I said. 'Compared to me you're the Sahara Desert!'

'Do you know what "sahara" means in Arabic?' Pete said. 'Desert. It means desert. True. So when we say "Sahara Desert" what we're really saying is "Desert Desert". How about that?'

'I'm gonna kill him,' I said to Angie.

Angie pulled herself together and unlaced my fingers. I dropped the grill into the water. It sank without trace.

'Now the sack,' she said. 'Pete, get in here.'

'No chance,' said Pete.

'PETE!'

He splashed in, scowling. 'This is all your fault, McCue. You and that stupid goose of yours.'

SSSSSSSsssssssSSSSSSSSsssssss

'You still here?' he said.

I stood back while Angie guided Pete's hands into the drain and he grabbed the sack, whimpering.

'Well, pull it, pull it!' she said to him.

'What do you think I'm trying to do, pluck its feathers one by one?'

But he pulled a bit harder, and pulled again, and once more, and then – SPLASH!

Over he went, on his back, the sack on top of him. 'Well done, Pete.' I grabbed the sack before it

133

floated away. Pete just lay there, spluttering and thrashing about.

Angie and I went to the door. 'People,' she said, looking out.

There were two of them, a couple, plus a silly little dog, wasting their lives looking in a closed shop window. In a minute they mooched off, but not before the dog had cocked his leg at the window to show what he thought of the display.

'To the tree!' Angie said when their heels had clicked away to nothing.

Dodging the two roving lenses, we dragged the sack across the square, leaving a wet sacky trail for Pete to follow when he stopped doing the backstroke in the Ladies.

'Hetty?' I said when we got to the tree. 'Are you with us or back there having a paddle with Pete?'

SSSSS$_{SS}$

'Sounds a bit beaked off,' said Angie.

'She's not the only one. So where did we go wrong yesterday?'

'We were facing the wrong way.'

'No, no, can't have been,' I said. 'That branch definitely hung over the house, I remember it vividly.'

'You vividly remember the wrong branch. The one hanging over the toilets is not the one that hung over the farmhouse. Looks the same 'cos it's about the same size, same model, but it's not the one. They lopped off the branch we were looking for when they built the square round the tree to show how much they care about nature.'

'How do you know which one got lopped?'

'Remember the last time we worked for old Brooky, when we went up to the house to plead for our wages? His goose – Hetty, as we now know – came at us like we were Jehovah's Witnesses or something. Half terrified us.'

'More than half,' I said.

'And when she flew at us I fell over this great root.'

'What great root?'

'This great root.'

We looked at the great root at the base of the tree. Most of it was inside the railings but there was a little warning sign near the bit they couldn't

135

get in. The little warning sign said: MIND THE ROOT.

'And this root,' Angie said, 'pointed to the very room where Mr Brook and Hetty played Scrabble in their bedsocks on chilly nights.'

'And now it's pointing at a flowerbed. Which is why you wanted me to bring the spade.'

'Right. But it's a bit exposed, so we'll have to watch those cameras. Dash out, dig, dash for cover when a camera comes, dash out, dig, dash for cover when a cam—'

'What's Pete up to?' I said.

Pete had finally quit the Ladies and was sauntering across the square like a tourist whose luggage has gone to the Bahamas without him. Wet footprints followed him. The cameras took it in turns to sweep across him. We shouted at him to cover his face, and get a move on before he was broadcast to the entire world by satellite.

'I'm past caring!' he shouted back.

Angie had already told Pete her idea so it didn't need to be repeated when he eventually joined us in hiding.

'But we don't know for certain that Hetty wants

to be buried in a flowerbed,' I said. 'I mean she hasn't actually *said*, has she.'

'So ask her,' said Ange.

'Hetty,' I said to a nearby patch of empty air, 'now I want you to think carefully before you answer, because I don't want you wrecking my reputation at *The Dorks* again. Or my room. See that flowerbed over there? That's where your old living room was. Now what I want you to tell us is: do you...want us...to bury your remains...there?'

SSSSsss

'Is that a yes or a no?' Angie whispered.

'Was that a yes or a no, Hetty?'

SSSSSSsssss

'Any questions?' I said to the others.

There were no questions, even from Pete, but that could be because he was too depressed to speak.

CHAPTER SEVENTEEN

After making sure that the entire local constabulary hadn't suddenly ridden their bikes into the square to take notes (and that the cameras were looking the other way) Angie and I rushed to the flowerbed. As I had the spade it was me who took first dig.

'Camera's coming,' Angie said after two strokes.

We trotted back to the tree, where we'd left the sack with Pete who seemed to want to spend his life there, dripping.

'Come on, Pete,' I said. 'One for all and all for lunch?'

'I'm not happy,' he said. 'I'm wet and I'm uncomfortable and the creases have fallen out of my jeans.'

'You *like* creases in your jeans?'

'Doesn't everyone?'

'Camera's gone,' said Ange.

I dashed out again, with her riding my heels.

'Pete!' I hissed.

He drifted after us and stood wringing his pockets out and mumbling as I dug some more.

'Whew,' I said. 'Hot work.'

'You've dug six centimetres,' said Ange.

'Ground's hard.'

'Pete, you take a turn.'

Pete took the spade and turned it over a couple of times as if he'd never seen one before.

'Camera's coming,' I said.

Pete threw the spade in the air and ran for cover like a madman. We followed, not quite as frantically. Those cameras were not fast swivellers.

'I have an idea,' Angie said under the tree.

Pete groaned. 'Just what we need, another idea.'

'It's this. You don't dig, Pete, you just stand here and tell us what the cameras are doing.'

'I like it,' said Pete, cheering up immediately. 'Camera's gone.'

Angie and I dashed out. I started digging again. She snatched the spade from me – 'Give me that!' – and did practically the whole job herself between runs. She didn't hang about either, just got on with it, no hassle, no complaints, no sweat, even under

139

the arms so far as I could tell. Angie Mint, a girl! What a waste.

When the hole was big enough we dropped the sack in and covered it over in double-quick time.

'What about flowers?' Angie said. 'She ought to have flowers.'

'She's got flowers,' said Pete, who was getting it together again at last and running out and back with us. 'She's in a bed of them.'

'Yeah, but look at the state of it.'

We looked at the state of the flowerbed. It wasn't as colourful as it should have been, being as there weren't many flowers in it. We took in the other flowerbeds round the square. Ditto. It was flower pinching season and they were all a little low on stock.

'Let's gather some up,' Angie said.

We raided the other flowerbeds and replanted a fair selection over Hetty's grave between camera swivels.

'Snag,' said Pete, right back on form now.

'Must you keep *saying* that?' I growled.

'Yes, but look. There are so many flowers over Hetty now, and so few everywhere else, that someone's bound to want to know what's down there.'

I hated to admit it, but he was right. So we took a lot of the flowers out again and − dodging the cameras − re-replanted them all over the place so no one would get suspicious.

When we'd finished, I said: 'Shouldn't we say something?'

'How about "Let's get outta here"?' said Pete.

'No, I mean some sort of…prayer or something.'

'I've been saying prayers ever since we arrived.'

'For Aunt Hetty.'

'A prayer for a goose?' he said. 'Gimme a break.'

'Well not a prayer exactly, just a few words. As a way of saying goodbye.'

'I think "Goodbye Hetty" says it all.'

'No, Jiggy has a point,' said Angie. 'This is a big moment in her life after all.'

'In her *life*?' said Pete.

'Camera coming,' I said.

We ran for cover. While we waited for the camera to move off I asked if anyone had anything to write with.

'I've got a felt-tip,' Angie said.

141

I took the felt-tip. 'Any paper?'

'Not this side of the Ladies,' said Ange.

'Camera's going,' said Pete.

'Hang on, I'm going to write something for Hetty. Turn round, Pete.'

'What for?'

'Just do it.' I spread my snot-stiffened hanky across his back and started to write. I didn't let them see till I'd finished.

'That's not right,' Pete said then.

'I know it's not *right*, I've adapted it for the occasion.'

'It doesn't fit the occasion.'

'Well it's short notice, you got any better ideas?'

He hadn't. Nor had Angie. 'It'll have to do,' she said. 'Hang around here much longer and we'll be released on Blu-ray, with a commentary and theme tune.'

We went back to the flowerbed, where we gathered in a solemn row of three and I held up my hanky and we read the immortal lines I'd arranged round the hard little black bits.

'Hey diddle-diddle
The cat did a piddle

A cow pat fell off the moon
The little dog barked to see such fun
And the goose flew away too soon.'

And then the most amazing thing happened. Just as we finished my farewell to Aunt Hetty there was this incredible noise from overhead. Naturally we looked up. And saw a flock of geese flying across the sky in this great V-shape.

'Now that,' Pete said, 'is what I call a coincidence.'

As they flew the geese flapped their wings so slowly you wondered how they stayed up there. Their necks were stretched right out, and their beaks made this sound, like a cross between a pack of hounds chasing a fox and a bunch of cracked old bells. I think I said 'Wow'.

'Twenty-four,' Angie breathed in my ear.

'Uh?'

'There's twenty-four of them. Eleven on one side, twelve on the other, plus the one in front making the point of the V. Twenty-four.'

HONK!

We grabbed hold of one another. That was one loud honk. And close. 'Hetty…' one of us said, or perhaps it was all of us.

HONK!

Not quite so loud this time, and up a bit. Then there it was again.

HONK!

And again, and again, and again. And each time invisible Hetty honked she did it a bit further away, a bit higher up the sky.

HONK! **HONK!** **HONK!** **HONK!**

'Awesome…' Pete murmured.

The shadow of a flying goose had appeared, very high up, approaching the V-shaped formation.

'Go on, girl,' I said. 'Go on, you can do it.'

'Twenty-five!' Angie laughed as Hetty clicked into place at the tail-end of the shorter line.

'Awesome,' said Pete again.

'Awesome,' said Angie.

'Awesome,' said I, and hoisted the spade to wave goodbye to the dear old goose.

CHAPTER EIGHTEEN

As we approached the back gate we heard music. Well, music. Sad Golden Oldie stuff so ancient that Noah danced to it with a hippo in the Ark. We opened the gate. I stashed the spade in the shed. We went round the 'L'. Audrey Mint and Oliver Garrett and Dad were on the patio admiring Mum's rockery. Dad obviously hadn't been to look at the Rodadoodah lately because he was smiling. All three of them were in their best clothes and all clean and shiny. Unlike us. They noticed this. So did Mum when she trotted out of the house five seconds later.

'Jiggy. I don't believe what I'm seeing!'

I held my hands up. I'd had it with explanations.

'Well whatever you've been up to you can go right upstairs this minute and wash. All of you. And you,' she said, glaring at me in particular, 'can change out of those *filthy* things.'

'Be glad to lose the sweater,' I said.

'You'll lose the lot. Your other jeans are in your wardrobe.'

'I can't change my jeans. Then I'll be the only neat one.'

'He has a point, Peg,' said Audrey. 'Unless you think we should take the other two home to change too...?'

Mum threw her bottom lip out. 'The meal's about ready.'

'Oh, leave 'em be,' my dad said. 'They've looked worse.'

Mum tossed some daggers at him but he ducked and she gave in.

'All right, but give yourselves a *good* wash. And be sharp about it, we're eating in five minutes!'

We went upstairs. I ran along the landing and threw my bedroom door back. 'Hetty?'

No answer. And the room felt different somehow. Gooseless. I could live with that.

'Gone!'

'And good riddance,' Pete said. 'I never *ever* want to see another goose, alive or dead.'

'Nor me,' said Ange.

We went to the bathroom. I looked at the taps

147

over the sink, decided it would be a shame to make the nice shiny handles dirty, and went back to my room where I finally found a use for Roger the gorilla, brushing off earth and other gunge with his long stupid arms. I was just kicking my gran's horrible sweater back under the bed when Mum called.

We went down, past the kitchen where the old dear was slaving away all on her own. 'Smells great, Mum,' I said to cheer her up. 'Hope it's chips.'

'It's not,' she said, miserable as sin.

We went out to the back garden.

'You three look very pleased with yourselves,' Oliver said.

'That's 'cos we're young and have our whole lives ahead of us,' Pete said, 'and you're old and you've had yours.'

Oliver gave him a nasty grin. 'Cheeky little B.'

'Have you heard the news?' my dad said to us.

'What news?'

He glanced at Audrey and Oliver. 'Can I tell them or do you want to?'

Oliver put his arm round Aud, still grinning. 'Go ahead, Mel.'

Pete clutched his head. 'Oh no, they're gonna get *married*.'

A strangled sound came from Angie. 'They can't do that. Then you and I would be related. Almost...brother and sister.'

A dozen freckles jumped off Pete's nose in alarm. 'You can't be best mates with your sister, it's impossible!'

Dad and Aud and Oliver had picked up on some of this and were chuckling like billy-o.

'No, no, no,' Oliver said. 'We wouldn't be daft enough to get married.'

Aud lurched away from him. 'No, we'd never do something as daft as *that*.'

'Whew,' said Pete and Angie and slapped palms.

'They're going to buy a house on the estate,' Dad said. 'Just across the road from us. We're all going to be neighbours again!'

More freckles popped off Pete's nose. 'You mean move? Move from Borderline Way?'

'Don't worry, Pete,' Mum said, looking out of the back door. 'We know a good behavioural psychologist who no longer has a picture over his chair. It's ready, everyone.'

The Golden Oldies rubbed their hands together and stampeded into the house.

'It's not *so* bad on the estate,' I said as we trailed after them. 'Once you get used to the newness and all.'

'Yeah, but I've lived on Borderline Way all my life,' Pete said.

'So had I, but I made it out of there and survived – just.'

'And we'll all be able to go to school together again,' Angie said.

Pete grunted. 'Better than getting related to one another, I s'pose.'

'Million times better than *that*,' said Ange.

We went indoors. The dining room looked a treat. Mum had really done a job there. Napkins in wooden rings and bright new cutlery and table-mats and dishes of veg and sauces and stuff. No chips. Dad was already in his place at one end of the table and Audrey and Oliver sat on one side, with the three chairs opposite them meant for us Musketeers. There was a bit of a scuffle while we jostled one another for the best seats. Angie got the middle one and smacked our arms till we stopped trying to get her out of it.

'All set, everyone?' Mum bawled from the kitchen.

'All set!' we all bawled back.

She came in carrying this huge silver platter that I hadn't seen before, with this huge silver dome on it.

'What is it, Mum? Chicken?'

'Wait and see.'

'Turkey? Can't be turkey, it's summer.'

She set the silver platter down in the space she'd left for it in the middle of the table.

'Hope you all like this. Otherwise it's back to the tin opener.'

Six heads leaned forward, twelve nostrils twitching in anticipation as Mum lifted the silver dome. And there it was, our house-warming dinner. Big, plump, steaming, and so tender-looking you could almost taste it already. Three grown-ups slapped their lips and reached for their knives and forks so they wouldn't have to waste any time when it was on their plates.

'Mum,' I said nervously. 'Mum, it's not...it's not a...?'

'It's a goose, darling,' Mum said. 'I don't think

151

you've ever had roast goose befo... Jiggy?'

My chair hit the wall behind me as I jumped up. *Splat*.

'What's up with you?' Dad said in surprise.

Two more chairs hit the wall. *Splat*. *Splat*. Pete and Angie were also on their feet.

'Angie!'

'Pete, what the hell are you playing at?'

Hands over our mouths, skin the colour of old broccoli, we broke all records for table-to-door sprinting, hoofed it along the hall, past the kitchen, out the back door. We made it to the patio only just in time, where we threw ourselves gratefully on to my mother's terrific new rockery.

'One for all and all for luuuuuunnnn...'

We almost got it out, almost but not quite. Got something else out instead. Mum didn't appreciate that when she saw. Nor did the others. You know the way parents stick together at times like that, gang up on you because they're bigger and fatter and pay the pocket money. Mum said she'd never be able to look at that rockery again without seeing the three of us sprawled across it heaving into it like there was no tomorrow. I felt the same, but for me it was one of those great moments. The Three Musketeers, side by side, us against the world. Pals, mates, chums. Buds to the bitter end.

CHAPTER NINETEEN

Guess what. The local paper just came through the door, and right there on the front page there's a picture of this kid at the shopping centre. He's got flowers on his shoulders and this lunatic grin on his face as he looks up, and because he's waving this spade in the air (which looks like a weapon the way he's holding it) you have to believe he's going to destroy something. And he's wearing this horrible sweater with a word as big as a bus on the chest. The word is JIGGY. The caption under the photo says:

THE BROOK FARM VANDAL.
DO YOU KNOW THIS BOY?

Hey. Some days you can't win whatever you do.

Jiggy McCue

Look out for more JiGGY in 2010!

RuDiE DuDiE

A new drama teacher arrives at Ranting Lane School. Is Jiggy really going to have to play Bottom in the school production of *A Midsummer Night's Dream*?

And introducing a brand-new series...

JiGGY'S GENES

...in which we meet a whole host of Jiggy's ancestors and discover that, through centuries past, there have *always* been Jiggy McCues!

Don't miss the first book,

JiGGY'S MiGHTY BALLS

where we meet a 13th century Jiggy...

Don't miss
the next exciting
JIGGY adventure...

NuDiE
DuDiE

TURN THE PAGE
TO READ THE BEGINNING...

CHAPTER ONE

Did you ever have a dream where there are people all around you and suddenly you're naked? I mean without a thing on. Totally starkers. Just you, no one else. Well count yourself lucky it was only a dream. Imagine if it happened in real life. Like it did to me.

It started the day Tony Baloney came to my school. Tony Baloney isn't his real name. I can't tell you his real name because he's quite famous. He's an actor in this TV soap about...

No, better not tell you that either, or you might guess who I'm talking about. Tony Baloney, under his real name, used to go to Ranting Lane School. He's the only ex-Ranting Laner who ever made a name for himself, even though it's the name of someone who speaks words written by other people and moves the way other people tell him. Think about it. There you are, a fully-evolved humanicus beingus, with the ability to walk, speak, hum, scratch and cut your own toenails, and you get famous for doing as you're told. And for this job, for being a flesh-and-blood dummy, you get paid a fortune, get your picture in the papers, and get asked to visit your old school to tell the kids that money and fame aren't all they're cracked up to be, which means that on top of everything else you're a bad liar.

And guess what. Guess whose mother is such a big drooling fan that she tells her only son that if I ever want to eat or wear an ironed shirt again I have to get the prat's autograph in my father's *Help the Aged* autograph book.

So there I am, lunch break, the great Jiggy McCue, waiting with all these girls at the bottom of the steps from the main building, while Tone Balone stands at the top signing little books and scraps of paper. The Star has hair that looks like it came out of a box marked Bozo Hair, and a tan that has to have started life in a tin labelled Boot Polish, and teeth that obviously glow in the dark and startle moths. 'It's great to see you,' he says to every fan one after the other, and as they go he says: 'Keep watching the show!'

At the top of the steps, as close as she can get to Baloney without tearing his shirt off and chewing his chest hair (probably fake), is Miss Weeks, our Deputy Head. She's all shy and girly, fingers twitching like they'll fall off if they don't touch him soon. I'm the only boy. The only male. And anyone who didn't know the real reason I'm there would think that I too am a fan of this git. It wouldn't have been so bad if Pete and Angie had been there. We could have made a big joke of all this. But they wouldn't come, even when I offered them money. So much for solidarity.

Miss Weeks saw me, and smiled, as if to say, 'So you're a fan too!' and I wanted to melt into the tarmac. But then someone came out of the building and said Miss W was wanted on the phone, and she excused herself and went in. Now it was just me and the adoring fans. I looked around for some sort of distraction, anything, not fussy, and saw someone standing next to me who hadn't been there a minute earlier.

This wasn't a Ranting Lane pupil. She

was a grown-up, and she had this short spiky hair and short spiky nose. She wore jeans that turned to rags just below the knee, and a T-shirt that screamed SAY NO, without saying what to. She stared up the steps at the Big Soap Star with this strange mixed expression, like she wanted to bury an adoring bread knife in his heart. She must have felt my eyes on her, because she glanced my way. The look in her eyes made me jump. They were so dark, yet bright too. If witches were real, I thought, this one would be chief cauldron-stirrer.

I cleared my throat. 'Fan?' I asked.

Instead of answering my friendly question she de-glanced and shoved through the girls to the top of the steps. Tony Baloney was surprised to find an adult suddenly at the head of the queue, but he said, 'Hi,' like he said to everyone, 'I'm Tony Baloney, and you are...?'

'Your number two fan,' she tells him. 'Ophelia.'

For a sec there's panic in TB's eyes. But then he realises that Ophelia is her name, not a wish.

'Great to see you, Ophelia,' he says. 'Er...number two fan?'

'Seeing you in the flesh,' she replies, 'I know that you are your number one fan.'

Tony Baloney smiles, but it's a wobbly sort of smile. 'Do you have something for me to sign?'

'No,' she says. 'I brought you a present.'

'A present?'

She handed him a blue oblong box. 'You didn't acknowledge the other things I sent you,' she says. 'So when I heard you were coming to Ranting

Lane I thought I'd put this in your hands personally. That way I'd *know* you received it.'

There was something about the word 'know', the way she said it, that made the fans on the steps stop talking and a frown appear on Tony Baloney's brow.

'You've sent other things?'

'A black silk shirt, embroidered slippers, an electric fan,' Ophelia says.

'Electric fan?'

'It was a joke. A fan from a fan?'

'Oh yes. Ha-ha. Very good.'

'You don't remember getting it, do you?' Ophelia says. 'Or the other things.'

'Of course I do,' says Tony Baloney. 'But I receive an awful lot of things from fans...'

'Well now you have another thing,' she says, with a voice so icy you'd think we'd been swallowed up by a sudden iceberg.

T-Bal opens the blue oblong box. He blinks. Then he stares at what he sees, like he's having trouble believing his eyes.

'It's a pen,' Ophelia explains.

'Excellent,' Tony says. 'Thank you. I'll treasure it.'

'You're not supposed to treasure it,' the spiky fan snaps. 'You're supposed to write with it.' She sounds very angry.

'I will,' says Tone, giving her the sparkly old Baloney smile. 'As soon as my present pen runs out.'

'Oh, *sure* you will,' Ophelia says, spinning round and pushing her way down the steps. She walks quickly across the playground to the gates.

Just before Tony B closes the blue oblong box and drops it in his jacket pocket I think I hear him mutter, 'Cheap rubbish,' but I could be wrong about that. He turns the brilliant Baloney teeth on the next fan, a smaller one, who offers him the back of an envelope. Halfway through dashing off his moniker he stops. 'Damn. My pen's dried.' He frowns around. 'Anyone happen to have a...?' But then his frown clears. 'Oh, but I have a spare, don't I?'

And at the very moment he reaches into his pocket for the blue oblong box he's just been given, this stupendously stupid idea trampolines into my feeble excuse for a mind. *Lend him your pen. Mum'll love to think this wally used your pen to write his crummy name for her!*

I sprang into action. 'Use mine, use mine!'

Tony Baloney's hand freezes in his pocket and comes out empty. 'OK. Thanks.' He reaches down, over the heads of the fans, and takes my pen — just as the bell for the end of lunch break goes.

The fans on the steps started to get agitated right away. When the school bell goes it means GET TO CLASS AT ONCE, not GET TO CLASS AS SOON AS YOU'VE GOT SOME BIG-HEAD'S AUTOGRAPH. Tony Baloney wasn't bothered that the bell had gone. He carried on writing at his usual speed, one soapy signature after another, with my pen. As soon as he finished each one, the fan snatched it off him and ran to class. I would have gone too – not run though, running isn't cool – but he had my pen and I couldn't take it back after lending it to him.

The minutes clunked by. The playground had gone absolutely silent. Two more girlie fans to go, but these were bigger girls, who could probably stand up to the teachers. They took their time, chatting with Tony like they were thinking of kidnapping him and feeding him Turkish Delight till the ransom cheque arrived.

But at last they went and it was my turn. I was about to hand over the *Help the Aged* autograph book when the Big Baloney reached into his pocket and took out the blue oblong box.

'Here,' he said. 'Present for you.'

He seemed to have forgotten that I'd seen Spiky give it to him a short while before.

'No, it's OK,' I said. 'Really.'

'I insist,' he said, shoving the box in my hand like it was something he'd just fished out of the toilet. 'Now I must run.' He winked at me. 'I can't believe I came back to this dump voluntarily. Don't quote me!'

He didn't run, but he didn't hang about either. He was down the steps and across the playground in a flash, climbing into his sporty red car in the teachers' car park. I stood at the top of the steps watching him go and wondering how, after all that, I'd failed to do what my mother had sent me there for.

Get the stiff's autograph.

I was about to enter the building with a weary sigh when the doors flew back and Miss Weeks leapt into my arms. She seemed quite startled about this. The farewell cuddle she'd been looking forward to hadn't been with me. She looked so disappointed to see the Star's exhaust fumes rising into the distance that you could have mistaken her face for an apple crumble.

But Miss Weeks was lucky. She might have missed a smooch with a smoothie, but she wasn't going to get a rollicking from her mother for not getting his autograph. In a minute she'd turn around and march back to normal life without any other big deals jumping into her path and spitting at her. Unlike me, she wasn't hours away from the most embarrassing pair of days of her life.

And I didn't even get my own pen back!

CHAPTER TWO

I did get one thing out of that autograph session, though. Detention. I'd kind of expected it when the bell went and I couldn't get to class. Last time I was late for one of his classes Face-Ache Dakin told me that if I was late for the next one it would be detention – and I was eight minutes late for the next one.

'But sir,' I said when he proved as good as his rotten word, 'I already have detention tonight with Mr Hurley.'

'Well now you have one on Monday as well, with me,' Face-Ache said. 'The way you're going, Master McCue, you'd better keep your diary free for some years to come.'

After school I went straight to Mr Hurley's room. Mr Hurley is our History teacher. He is not greatly loved. If there's one thing Mr H enjoys more than boring the sporrans off us with totally uninteresting things that have happened at some point in the past ten thousand years or so, it's dishing out detentions. Mine was for answering back. Answering back? I was just replying. You can't talk to that man.

I wasn't the only one in detention. My archest of enemies Bryan Ryan also filed in, along with Ian Pitwell, Terry Toklas and Martin Skinner. Skinner was a surprise. He's such a creepy-crawler that you can't imagine him ever getting in trouble. Turned out he'd asked to be there – yes, asked! – because he was writing an essay called *Being in Detention* and he needed to see what happened in it.

When Mr Hurley came in, Ryan said, 'You're late, sir. Detention!' Hurley asked him if he wanted to spend the entire evening there, and Ryan said he'd love to but his mum needed help with the sausage rolls.

'Sausage rolls?' said Hurley.

Read the rest of
Nudie Dudie
to find out what happens next!

READ ALL THE HiLARiOUS
JiGGY McCUE BOOKS!

All priced at £5.99

Orchard books are available from all good bookshops,
or can be ordered direct from the publisher:
Orchard Books, PO BOX 29, Douglas IM99 1BQ
Credit card orders please telephone 01624 836000 or fax 01624 837033
or visit our website: www.orchardbooks.co.uk
or email: bookshop@enterprise.net for details.

To order please quote title, author and ISBN and your full name and address.
Cheques and postal orders should be made payable to "Bookpost plc."
Postage and packing is FREE within the UK
(overseas customers should add £1.00 per book)

Prices and availability are subject to change.

Dedicated to all of those beautiful

people

who have chosen to stand in love for

God's best...

-The healing of their marriages-

Husbands, love your wives, just as Christ loved the church and gave himself up for her to make her holy, cleansing her by the washing with water through the word, and to present her to himself as a radiant church, without stain or wrinkle or any other blemish, but holy and blameless. In the same way, husbands ought to love their wives as their own bodies. He who loves his wife loves himself. After all, no one ever hated his own body, but he feeds and cares for it, just as Christ does the church – for we are members of his body. "For this reason a man will leave his father and mother and be united to his wife, and the two will become one flesh." This is a profound mystery – but I am talking about Christ and the church. However, each one of you also must love his wife as he loves himself and the wife must respect her husband.

Ephesians 5:25–33(NIV)

Then and Now

The manuscript for the book you hold in your hand was prepared years ago and was my first book-writing effort. Despite many additional books, *Prodigals Do Come Home* remains our most requested. Each time my wife, Charlyne, and I consider retiring this book, something happens to show us clearly that the Lord is continuing to use this story.

You will be reading about divorce and our three children. They are grown now, with spouses of their own. Additionally, many grandchildren are now in the picture. We are thankful to God to be living within a few miles of all our children and grandchildren.

In the wee hours of the morning, when God first planted the idea for this book into my heart, we had been remarried for three years. There was no Rejoice Marriage Ministries, nor did either of us envision ever birthing a marriage ministry.

I had been called to preach in 1974. Our family moved away to Bible college, and I received additional ministerial education by correspondence. I began running from God's call on my life, I reasoned that He had enough poor preachers and needed more tithing laymen. Even though I returned to funeral service, the Lord did not release me from His call on my life. In retrospect, I now understand that everywhere the Lord took me, including five years as a hospice chaplain, was in preparation for founding a marriage ministry.

Two months after our divorce was final God spoke to Charlyne and reminded her that He had not given up on me, but she had. On that same Sunday, my wife took a stand with the Lord, praying for our marriage restoration. Over two years later, her prayers were answered when I went to Charlyne's office window and invited her to lunch. As I sat across from her that day, the Holy Spirit spoke to me and convicted me of the terrible mistake I had made. Our pastor remarried us that same afternoon.

While we were divorced, Charlyne had asked the Lord to allow her to help one other woman avoid the mistake she had made. God's blessings to a wife who was faithful in her stand, has now expanded that "one woman" she prayed to help into countless thousands. Her teachings recorded live at Rejoice Pompano Beach Bible Study are played by thousands around the world.

When *Prodigals Do Come Home* was written, neither of us had heard of email. Now, each day *Charlyne Cares,* an email of encouragement based on God's Word, is sent to men and women around the world who are standing with God and refusing to give up on their marriages.

Looking back, I thought I was fulfilling my responsibilities to God and to other hurting families by writing the manuscript for this book. This was my answer for the divorce dilemma. Since we had no idea of being in ministry, the manuscript was assigned to Dr. Bob Christensen at Covenant Marriage Ministry.

Following the publication of *Prodigals Do Come Home,* Charlyne and I began to receive phone calls at home from people, many of whom had gone to great lengths to locate us, since only our names and some geographic references appeared in the *Prodigals* story. In fact, every Steinkamp in Florida began to receive calls. People only wanted to ask, "Is it true? Are you still together? Is there hope for my marriage?"

We began to correspond with people across the nation. One evening, a few months later, our first newsletter, two typed pages, was prepared. It was copied at eight copies a minute on a small machine that one of my hospice patients had donated to us. We only made sixty copies and probably have some of them still left.

That first newsletter bore the name Rejoice Marriage Ministries, the same name the Lord had given to both Charlyne and me while we were divorced. (I had thought that Rejoice Marriage Ministries was going to be a divorce recovery ministry, until Jesus came by!)

The rest of the Rejoice report is history, as God has led us, built His ministry and used it to lead thousands of couples around the world to marriages restored on the solid rock of Jesus Christ.

For eleven years, Dr. Bob, who we refer to as the "Grandfather of Rejoice Marriage Ministries," has published this book and graciously provided copies for us. In December, 2002 the manuscript was assigned back to us, allowing Rejoice Marriage Ministries to now print *Prodigals Do Come Home* for you.

Due to time constraints, it may be more difficult for you to talk to us now, but here are the answers to those first questions people were asking. Yes, it is true. Yes, we are still together. Yes, there is hope for your marriage. It is found not in what we do, but in the Lord Jesus Christ. May God bless you as you read our story.

Bob Steinkamp

So do not throw away your confidence; it will be richly rewarded. You need to persevere so that when you have done the will of God, you will receive what he has promised. **Hebrews 10:35-36**

Introduction

When I saw the fear and confusion in that man's eyes, I recognized the assignment God had for me. The hour was approaching midnight. My duties as a funeral director had taken me to one of our community hospitals. I was in the emergency department when he walked in, bent over, holding his abdomen. Although I didn't intend to eavesdrop, I soon found myself listening to soft-spoken answers to the routine questions being posed by the admittance personnel. The conversation went something like this:

"I have pain, a lot of pain in my stomach. I live alone, and I was afraid it might be serious. My next of kin? I don't know. My wife and I are separated and getting a divorce. My children are small and live with my wife. My parents are older, and they're upset with me about the divorce. Can I give you my boss's name? Sure, I work for..."

"Yes, I have insurance, but I can't pay you anything tonight. I'm broke. My paycheck doesn't go far enough, between helping support my children and paying for the room I rent.

"My religion? I don't know. I'm not going to church right now because of the divorce. No one there knows what to say to me. Just put down Protestant, I guess.

"My physician? I guess I need you to find one for me. Our family has always gone to the same doctor, but my wife is going to him now because she's been sick a lot since we separated. He would probably be uncomfortable treating both of us."

As I walked out into the warm Florida night air, I saw the car he had driven to the hospital. Perhaps symbolic of how this man was feeling, his automobile sat alone in the emergency parking area, appearing as a testimony to better days. The four-door sedan was in need of repair, probably now being passed over because of limited funds. A bumper sticker from a local church was displayed right next to the one proclaiming this message: My Child Is An Honor Student.

Now, because of divorce, this man considered himself without either family or church. I wanted to run back inside the hospital, put an arm around the shoulder of that hurting man and give words of encouragement.

Afraid that some wouldn't understand a funeral director befriending an emergency room patient, I drove away reflecting on what I observed. I recalled nights in my own life when my answers to a hospital secretary's questions would have paralleled those I just heard. Had my friend arrived at the hospital and stated that he was suffering from a terminal illness, one for which I knew the cure, no time would have been wasted in passing along all I knew about the illness. But because his illness was spelled d-i-v-o-r-c-e, I was hesitant to share my experience with him.

Our God, in His mercy, allowed our family to suffer the tragedy of divorce. My wife, Charlyne, and our three children and I have been there.

But there's good news. Our Lord restores marriages, regardless of impossible circumstances. My prayer is that the Holy Spirit may take this book and allow a few words penned by man to comfort and encourage you. My purpose is not to condemn, but to enlighten. My plea is that you will remain sensitive and open to God's provisions for troubled marriages.

Table of Contents

Then and Now

Introduction

Introducing Rejoice Marriage Ministries

Chapter One

The Prodigal

Then He said: "A certain man had two sons. And the younger of them said to his father, 'Father, give me the portion of goods that falls to me.' So he divided to them his livelihood." **Luke 15:11-12 (NKJV)**

Perhaps you're thinking that is a strange verse to introduce the first chapter of a book dealing with marriage and divorce. No, the application isn't about property settlement agreements, but rather about a lifestyle. This beautiful illustration of a restored relationship, told by Jesus two thousand years ago, came alive to me two years ago. Our Lord used that old story to change my life from a mess to a message.

The parable of the prodigal son isn't new to any of us. For many, it's one of those illustrations we have heard so many times that we tend to tune it out shortly after hearing its introduction.

Thirty years ago I would have objected had anyone suggested that my life would ever in any way be similar to that of the prodigal son. My bride and I were in our twenties. Our parents had been church friends. The backgrounds of our families were quite similar. Our goals and priorities were almost identical. Charlyne and I were both successful in our careers. We had purchased our first small home when we married. We anticipated the day we would have children, creating two sets of proud first-time grandparents. Although we weren't walking with the Lord, we attended the church where we had been married. I intended to live a good life, never venturing near a lifestyle similar to that of the prodigal. During the 1960's, divorce was something that happened to other people, so we never considered it would affect our happy family. It seemed that certain actions caused divorce, and my new wife and I were smart enough, perhaps even "religious" enough to stay away from those actions.

One cause of divorce that we don't hear much about is what some call the 40-20 divorce. A more appropriate name might be Satan's divorce. The couple reach their 40's, having been married about twenty years, and neither really seem to have put much effort into the relationship. One or both may not care if the marriage ends. If both were honest, one or the other has probably thought about how life might be better without his or her mate.

Most people, especially Christians, know enough to stay away from adultery, alcoholism, and the other problems that are often blamed for divorce. Few have ever heard that Satan hates marriage and uses subtle schemes to divide families. We all know families, even some in our own churches, who have divorced for no apparent reason. There really is a reason. The work of Christ is hindered in every way when a couple submits to divorce.

If you're reading this seeking biblical reasons to end a marriage, I'm afraid you'll be disappointed with this book. If you're seeking biblical reasons for marriage to another person after a divorce, I can promise that you'll be disappointed. The good news is that our God has a plan for you, your spouse, and your marriage that exceeds even that perfect life after divorce that prodigals often conjure in the mind's eye.

Volumes have been written and perhaps too many sermons delivered that take a legalistic look at the Bible's instruction on divorce and remarriage. Let's look at a condensation of the teachings of Jesus on the topic as found in the Gospel of Mark:

Some Pharisees came and tested him by asking, "Is it lawful for a man to divorce his wife?" "What did Moses command you?" he replied. They said, "Moses permitted a man to write a certificate of divorce and send her away." "It was because your hearts were hard that Moses wrote you this law," Jesus replied. "But at the beginning of creation God 'made them male and female.' 'For this reason a man will leave his father and mother and be united to his wife, and the two will become one flesh.' So they are no longer two, but one. Therefore what God has joined together, let man not separate." When they were in the house again, the disciples asked Jesus about this. He answered, "Anyone who divorces his wife and marries another woman commits adultery against her. And if she divorces her husband and marries another man, she commits adultery." Mark 10:2-12

Perhaps you'll recognize excerpts from this passage heard at most marriage ceremonies. One benediction goes as follows:

For this reason a man will leave his father and mother and be united to his wife, and the two will become one flesh.

Here's another:

Therefore what God has joined together, let man not separate.

One can only imagine the results if a minister asked to officiate at a second or third marriage selected different verses from that same text:

Anyone who divorces his wife and marries another woman commits adultery against her.

A benediction pronouncing *"and if she divorces her husband and marries another man, she commits adultery,"* might be more biblical even though quite a scene would probably ensue. We need to be careful not to take aim and fire shots at those who have been divorced and later married another person. Most of these people have suffered heartaches that we'll never know. Such couples, found in every church today, may have come to know God's perfect will for marriage later in life.

I'm thankful that God's grace is sufficient for every situation and that we have not been called to judge prior divorces. I feel very strongly that the Christian community has a responsibility to do everything possible to prevent additional divorces. For too long we have looked the other way as married friends have been separated by Satan. The price paid by divorced families has already been too great for us to refrain from becoming involved with helping them.

One morning recently I was waiting in the staff lounge of a local funeral home for a service to begin. There were four other men waiting with me. The subject of divorce came up, and we discovered that each of our five lives had been directly impacted by divorce. Sitting there, drinking coffee and talking, we probably sounded like a cross between a TV talk-show panel and a divorce support group. Although our stories differed, all shared a common trait. The cost of divorce on each of our lives had been great.

Paul, an elderly man, had been divorced many years ago. He recalled the separation and divorce as if it had all happened just recently. Dan had married a divorced woman with children. He told of the guilt he felt as he sat in another man's house with his wife and played with his children (his words, not mine). Dan described legal problems that had continued for years. Jack, a middle-aged business owner, continues to pay expensive child support, working hard to make his new business survive. Robert, the man who started the conversation, had been served with divorce papers just the day before after a two-year separation.

I shared my story of divorce and remarriage. Although one doubted that such an event could actually happen, I observed that none of these men condemned their former spouses or others who had been involved in their divorces. No one commented that I had made a mistake by my remarriage. As we shared, I reflected on the spiritual condition of each man. Although at least two would probably profess to be Christians, they do not have a daily walk with Jesus Christ. Had someone been available at the right time to share God's plan for one marriage for a lifetime, all five of our divorces may have been prevented. Had that happened, that coffee room could have been filled with five men whose lives showed the love of Christ. There would have been no reason for any of our divorces.

About now you're probably considering the exception clause, *"...except for marital unfaithfulness..."* found in *Matthew 5:32*. Nowhere does Scripture demand that one must divorce an unfaithful spouse. In addition, a divorce under such circumstances never legitimizes remarriage.

One of my favorite ways to spend a Saturday morning is to visit Port Everglades in nearby Fort Lauderdale and observe the cruise ships that arrive each weekend. I'm amazed at the amount of time the crews spend while in port working on lifeboats. They are painted, equipped, tested and always occupy a prominent place on the ships' decks. They're considered so important that shortly after each ship sails, a lifeboat drill is conducted for the passengers. Despite all that preparation, I have yet to see a single passenger sailing into the port in a lifeboat following a majestic cruise ship. The lifeboats are there in case the ship sinks, not so that the ship can sink. I see a parallel between lifeboats on cruise ships and marriage and divorce. Even when sailing gets rough on cruise ships, the passengers don't run for the lifeboats. That solution would only cause the passengers more problems. When a marriage goes through rough seas, we can't afford to run to the lifeboat of divorce. Although the lifeboat may be there, the cost of sailing it is just too great. Why not let our Jesus calm the seas for your ship instead of jumping into a lifeboat?

PUTTING FAITH INTO ACTION -

Consider, today, starting a personal journal. An inexpensive notebook can become a friend that listens to your fears and hopes without offering advice and without disclosing details to others. As your seas begin to smooth, you'll be looking back in amazement at where the Lord has taken you as you sought to find and do His will in your marriage. There's only one rule: write something in your journal every day. Although my wife wrote her journal to be personal, some of our closest times since remarriage have been when she shared with me a specific entry regarding her prodigal.

CHAPTER TWO
The Gathering

"And not many days after, the younger **son gathered all together***, journeyed to a far country, and there wasted his possessions with prodigal living."* **Luke 15:13 (NKJV)**
(emphasis mine)

One of the first steps for the individual preparing to leave for the far country is to gather their possessions together. Regardless of whether, like me, you're the prodigal, or one of those left behind, perhaps looking at the gathering process will help us understand what's taking place. For most prodigals, a mental gathering is taking place long before the first suitcase comes out of the closet.

A word of caution: If you've already seen something of yourself in these pages and have done some mental gathering, a plan for interruption of the thought cycle should take place immediately. A good scripture to recall might be *2 Corinthians 10:5:*

We demolish arguments and every pretension that sets itself up against the knowledge of God, and we take captive every thought to make it obedient to Christ.

For example, while walking through your living room your attention stops on a favorite chair. The thought crosses your mind that should anything ever happen to your marriage you would certainly want that item to be yours. There's no reason to feel you'll ever be leaving home, but the thought still takes place. A few days later someone at work mentions a new apartment complex with windows that overlook a lake. For just a moment you reflect on how comfortable you would be sitting in that favorite chair looking out over a beautiful lake. That evening, or possibly a few nights later, your wife has had a trying day. Her words to you seem a bit short. You recall the image of sitting in that chair, looking out across the lake. Somehow, your wife and her words don't find a place in your mental picture. From now on, every time a wave rocks the matrimonial boat, you allow your mind to sit in your chair in your apartment. The solution? Recognize that Satan destroys marriages and has just started the process to destroy yours. Every time that thought process starts, immediately recall a verse that claims the power of Christ over every thought.

Although we can't control every thought that crosses our minds, we can control how we dispel or cultivate the thoughts. A pastor friend once compared the process to being the manager of a hotel. Although the manager can't really control who walks through his lobby, he certainly can control to whom he rents his rooms. Let's hang out the *no vacancy* sign to any thought, regardless of how innocent, that would take our minds away from our marriages.

At some point in the separation and divorce process, a physical gathering by the prodigal takes place. This is one of the first opportunities for the mate being left behind to show unconditional love to the prodigal. In the parable, the prodigal asked for his portion. The Bible doesn't speak of a court fight to divide the portions as happens in many families today.

When your prodigal asks for particular items, try, if at all possible, to accommodate his (or her) requests. You should allow this for three reasons. First, remember that the prodigal's thought process isn't just right or the separation probably wouldn't be taking place at all. Your refusal to go to court to fight to keep the grinder on the work bench, as happened to a friend of mine, says something to your prodigal. Even though you may not detect it, most prodigals are overcome with guilt at this stage. Your refusal to fight over petty issues will only cause the prodigal to consider what he is doing to a loving family.

Secondly, since our memories are personal, the mate left behind doesn't know why the prodigal is making an issue over a small item. Allowing him to remove that item also demands he takes the memories of that item with him. When my wife and I separated, I demanded the coffeemaker. Although it was old at the time, I wanted it to be mine. Unfortunately, the thing refused to die, and I had to make coffee each morning for two years facing the same device that my wife had used to make coffee for several years. Many times, while waiting for coffee to brew, my mind would drift back to my family's home and those who still lived there.

Finally, do not be too concerned about what the prodigal gathers for his trip to the far country, because when our Lord returns your prodigal to you, those same items will return home. This morning my coffee was made in that same machine that had been to the far country and back. The difference today is that it was made in our home by the wife of my youth. Now I hope that old coffeemaker lasts forever because of the same memories.

Some spouses have trouble with the gathering for another reason. The spouse who is left behind can't stand the thought of another person having access to the item that had belonged to both of them and their once-happy family. Although it may be difficult to comprehend through your hurting, please accept this prodigal's testimony. That other person will never come near your former personal items without causing the prodigal to remember. I can't find the words to express the emotion that took place each time another person would approach my coffeemaker to make coffee. That causes a prodigal to do a lot of thinking.

I don't mean to imply it will be easy for you to watch your mate back a truck up to the door and remove items from the family residence. What some may forget is that it's really just as difficult for the one backing up the truck. It's one of the most difficult of some already difficult days. If the Lord had equipped each of us with a window into the heart, you would see that your prodigal, regardless of all outward appearances, is trembling inside. Please, on that day, allow God's love for you and His concern for your family to take the place of the hatred and bitterness toward him or her that Satan would desire you have. Without pressure, allow your unconditional love for your prodigal to be seen. Nothing hurts prodigals more than having the one left behind offer more than was demanded. Pray that God's Holy Spirit, our Comforter, would take the place of each item the prodigal removes from the home.

Many prodigals return to claim additional items from their home. Perhaps this should be seen as the first small victory for the one left behind. It's not that the prodigal needs those additional items to survive, perhaps it's more that he needs more security (and memories) of the marriage. Let this encourage you rather than discourage. Why? The prodigal had to return from the far country, at least for a moment to claim what he thought he needed. Don't question why your spouse, living on the tenth floor of an apartment building needs the family's only garden hose. Give it to him, knowing that he's taking along memories of washing the family car on Saturday afternoons, filling the wading pool for his children, and others that you can't imagine. His taking the hose has been a good day for you. After all, prodigals do come home.

PUTTING FAITH INTO ACTION -

During separation or divorce, most people either draw close to God or pull away from Him. Rather than blaming God for your situation, please allow Him to be your spouse during the time of separation from your mate. Perhaps it's been a long time since you prayed. Today, go to our Heavenly Father in prayer and let Him know how you feel. Your words are not important. Our God knows your heart. He is waiting to be your source of strength, comfort and supply for all your needs.

CHAPTER THREE

The Far Journey

*"'And not many days after, the younger son gathered all together, **journeyed to a far country**, and there wasted his possessions with prodigal living.'"* **Luke 15:13 (NKJV)** (emphasis mine)

Where did the prodigal go? Although we're not told the distance, it wasn't so far that he couldn't return home. Don't be discouraged by the distance to your prodigal's far country. The grace of God can reach around the world just as easily as around the block. We have a friend whose prodigal wife moved only two blocks away from the home he occupied with their two sons. Another friend's husband moved several thousand miles away.

My far country started out only twenty miles from our home. My first efficiency apartment was a few blocks outside the telephone company's local calling area. Perhaps long distance calls made me feel a long distance from home. A year later, still running from the one who loved me, I moved one hundred twenty miles in the opposite direction. Several months later, I moved forty miles in yet another direction.

Although the far country differs for each prodigal, all appear to have several common factors. Most prodigals attempt in varying degrees to maintain contact with their families. I would be wealthy if it were possible to recover long-distance phone charges for calls made with the intention of checking on my children. Although they were important to me, I really didn't expect to find them awake at 11 P.M. Calling at that time (because the rates were cheaper) meant I could speak with my wife. When you hear that your out-of-town prodigal is back in your home town, perhaps his sole reason is to be near his family for a while.

Most prodigals also re-establish their new surroundings in the far country to be similar to their family's home. One friend (with more money than most prodigals) hired an interior decorator to reproduce his former home in a new apartment. All I could afford was to reposition the bed in my efficiency so that I could look to the right and see the moonlight the same as I could do in my own bed at home. If you were able to look at the kitchen shelves in your prodigal's kitchen, you would probably find the same items as the family home.

Despite the prodigal's best attempts at physical reconstruction, he will never be able to create the desired image of his former home. The key to why his efforts fail are found in the Bible. When the prodigal was married, he and his spouse became **one flesh. Separation and divorce are futile attempts to divide that one flesh back into two separate people. God says that will not work.**

From time to time, I awake during the night with pain in my left elbow. It is not serious enough to require a trip to the doctor, but it is annoying. Although I hate to admit it, the discomfort is the type that goes along with reaching the mid-forties. Despite the inconvenience, I have never considered removing my left arm to end the pain. Our bodies are not made to function properly with an arm missing. I could get by, but life would never be the same. The prodigal's attempt to divorce a spouse is an attempt to remove part of his own flesh. The results can't be successful because it's contrary to God's perfect plan for His children.

Despite what you may hear, the far country is a lonely place for the prodigal. When he left for the far country, he probably left behind most or all of the couple's former friends. Unfortunately, he probably also left behind his church family. Prodigals frequently undergo job or even career changes while there.

We find the prodigal in a far country, his entire world has been turned upside down. He has left behind a family, friends, possibly a career. All he has taken are a few possessions, a lot of guilt, and the excess baggage of a failed marriage (so he thinks!), and he attempts to create a new life for himself.

The fortunate prodigal is the one who turns to his Creator for answers and soon finds the solution. Most prodigals, like myself, continue their feeble attempts to make it all work properly – all by themselves. We seem to reason somehow, that since others have gone through separation and divorce and have survived, we can also.

The prodigal is about to enter what some call the *act unlike yourself* stage. Although the solution will never be found except through Jesus Christ, the prodigal explores new directions looking for that which will bring meaning back to his now meaningless life. New clothing, a different hair style, a flashy sports car, or new traits enter the picture. Being unable to afford a sports car or much else, I dieted on my own and lost one hundred pounds during the first year. I had never before been able to accomplish this. The prodigal that had never entered a bar may now be seen in one on a regular basis. His speech may change. The prodigal who always retired at 10 P.M., now becomes a night owl.

About this time, the spouse at home begins to hear things about the prodigal, regardless of the distance to the far country. When Satan has a message to be delivered, there is always a messenger. The spouse is ready to forget it all, saying, "After all, he left me, so why should I want him back?" We have touched upon one of the first and often most difficult challenges for the person waiting at home. We must realize that people do gossip. Try to discount about ninety-nine percent of what you hear about your prodigal. A busybody needs more than being able to report that the prodigal has drawn closer to the Lord since he went to the far country.

Regardless of the circumstances involved, the spouse who can continue to exhibit unconditional love for the prodigal is one up on Satan and winning the battle. The true concept of unconditional love is love regardless of the circumstances. That comes only by personal experience. Unconditional love allows us to exhibit one of the ways of God Himself, in that we can hate the sin but continue to love the sinner.

Perhaps a word of caution is needed. Your prodigal is trying to live right side up in an upside down world. His emotions are playing constant tricks on him. The person at home needs to be prepared for getting clobbered by the prodigal's pendulum of emotion. His moods may swing very quickly from almost euphoria to total depression. The prodigal who calls home to check on his children and to tell his spouse how great everything is going is the same person who calls back an hour later trying to speak through tears and from the pit of depression.

Although some prodigals are better at masking emotions, the person waiting at home often becomes victim to kind, loving words, followed shortly by words of hate. Perhaps most devastating are broken dates and promises. Your prodigal plans to meet you for whatever reason, and then suddenly backs out or terminates the meeting without notice. Remember that although it's difficult for you at home, things are probably even rougher for your prodigal in the far country. When you are hurt by the prodigal's swaying emotions, allow the love of Christ to soften the harsh words. No matter the circumstances, look to Him through your tears to keep you walking in faith.

PUTTING FAITH INTO ACTION -

We all know people who seem to have a direct prayer line to Heaven. When they pray things happen. If you were in need of life-saving prayer today, who would you call? Please consider asking that person to become your prayer partner for your prodigal and your marriage. Perhaps the greatest compliment we can pay another person is to acknowledge their successful prayer life.

CHAPTER FOUR

The Prodigal In Want

"But when he had spent all, there arose a severe famine in that land, and he began to be in want." **Luke 15:14 (NKJV)**

If we could locate all the prodigals in all the far countries and poll them, I think we would find that their number one problem would be related to their finances. The cost of becoming a prodigal is simply too great.

I feel that financial problems rank at or near the top of Satan's list of schemes to defeat the separated family, especially the spouse waiting at home. Most families today find it difficult to make ends meet. When the prodigal leaves and attempts to establish a residence in the far country, many household expenses are doubled for the family. After a few months, the one at home is ready to give up because of money.

Since I'm not an expert on finance, I can't offer a single word of professional advice. I can, however, offer my family's personal experience on how to survive until the prodigal returns home. Perhaps we need to memorize **Philippians 4:19**:

And my God will meet all your needs according to his glorious riches in Christ Jesus.

It is important to note that the Bible doesn't say **can supply**, but rather **shall supply all your needs.** Our God, Who created all that is, certainly has the ability to meet the needs of families seeking to do His will by waiting for the prodigals to come home. Giving up on your one flesh mate because of finances is giving in to Satan's plan for your marriage.

Although the text promises that our Lord shall supply all our needs, it doesn't say that there won't be some real tests of our faith along the way. Our needs in financial matters will be supplied, but that doesn't excuse us from being fully responsible for our own finances. We are to be good stewards.

A spouse being responsible in finances is one of the greatest avenues of expression of unconditional love to the prodigal, even when he refuses to accept his share of the responsibility. Being responsible doesn't necessarily mean paying all the bills. It does mean staying in touch with creditors and paying as God provides, as well as keeping a firm hand on the money that is available.

When this prodigal left for the far country, like most, I left behind the family's bills. Although Charlyne and I agreed on child support amounts and each check reached her on time, there just wasn't enough money to pay the obligations. Realizing this, Charlyne wrote letters to each creditor before the final notices arrived. She explained our pending divorce and the reason for being unable to make full payment. She stated that she was accepting responsibility for the debt and would be making regular payments. She wrote to companies that had issued credit cards and promised not to use the credit card (something we should have done together a long time ago). Enclosed with each letter was a check. Depending on the size of the obligation, some checks were for only five dollars. Every company she wrote responded in a positive manner. Some even thanked her for having contacted them.

Some may think she did a stupid thing to take on this responsibility. I don't. Not only did she protect her credit rating, her actions caused me to ponder how she could be actually helping me when I had left the home. Later I discovered this was just a small part of her unconditional love for me. At the same time, Charlyne worked out a budget for the money she had available. After hearing reports from my children on her cuts, I realized our nation was missing out by not using her in Washington. The newspaper delivery was stopped, the air conditioning eliminated, cable television was reduced to basic service, and lunches were taken to school and work. Dinners remained nutritious but low-budget, and clothes were hung out to dry instead of using the clothes dryer.

There are two important concepts that need to be passed along. First, no matter how tight the budget, never rob God of His tithe. His perfect plan for you, your life, and your marriage is broken when His tithe is withheld from the local church. You can trust Him to meet your needs only when biblical principles of tithing are followed. People who are having real financial problems are sometimes people who are failing to tithe.

Secondly, never discuss your financial needs with anyone who is better off financially than you. Asking a wealthy church friend to pray for your needs may bring money, but it may short-circuit God's plan to bless you and may rob another person of God's opportunity for them to be a blessing to you. Talk to God about your financial needs. If you need to share your burden with another person, do so with someone who has less money than you.

Shortly after our divorce, the family's washing machine quit working. Charlyne didn't have money to get it repaired. After working all day, she made evening trips to a coin laundry. The need was shared only with Jesus. Within two weeks, a couple in the church approached Charlyne with a check for $100. Although their family had little money, they had received an unexpected check and felt led of the Lord to give it to Charlyne. The washing machine repair combined with the tithe came within twelve cents of the check's amount. A few weeks later that same couple was blessed with an unexpected check for $200.

Another word of caution: Be prepared for that inevitable day when you've cut expenses to the basics and are still having trouble paying bills. You may discover that your prodigal now appears to be living better than you. He doesn't show any sign of financial problems. Please don't allow Satan to use this to hinder your unconditional love for your prodigal. Once again, discount about ninety-nine percent of what you are hearing about his or her lifestyle. The changes are probably superficial and being financed by a new credit card.

An incident comes to mind from my own time in the far country. Although personal, I feel it should be shared if it can help another understand the prodigal. The setting was a Saturday evening early in February. The weather was cold, even for Florida. I decided to drop off Charlyne's child support check, since I was going to be passing through town that night. Reflecting on the event, I realize now that my good intentions lacked good judgment.

That afternoon I had attended a wedding with…(oh well)…a girlfriend from the church I attended after our divorce. After the wedding, we had dinner and had gone to a Christian concert. It was one of a concert series that Charlyne and I used to attend. I knocked on the door of my former home wearing a new gray suit and pink shirt. I had lost about 40 pounds and had styled my hair for the first time in my life. I was driving the girlfriend's customized van which had been parked a few doors away with my friend waiting inside.

Charlyne had answered the door wearing her favorite old robe. She had spent her Saturday night working on the bills, making token payments to creditors. The temperature inside was colder than outside as she had turned down the heat to save money. Her mouth dropped open when she saw the new me. Although she invited me inside, I could not stay since I had someone waiting for me. To this day, I still appreciate Charlyne not attempting to murder me on the spot.

What she didn't know was the suit, which cost $79 at a discount store, had been charged. The pink shirt had been purchased by the girlfriend. We were in her van because I didn't have gas money for my old car. The concert tickets had been obtained from a friend, and dinner was courtesy of the girlfriend's father. My hair was longer because I couldn't afford a haircut until next payday.

As I walked down the street to the waiting van, with the wife of my youth watching from the door of our home, I realized, perhaps for the first time, that I was wasting my substance with riotous living. By the way, the feature at the concert that evening had included a presentation of the parable of *The Prodigal Son.*

PUTTING FAITH INTO ACTION -

During some of the darkest times while living in the far country, I would turn on a Christian radio station and hear words to a song that seemed as though they had been sung just for me. Please try playing Christian music and let our Lord minister and comfort you in a special way.

CHAPTER FIVE

Feeding The Swine

"Then he went and joined himself to a citizen of that country, and he sent him into his fields to feed swine."
Luke 15:15 (NKJV)

About this time some may be saying, "That's fine for others, but my situation is so much more complicated." No marriage or family situation is too complicated or too messy for Jesus Christ to straighten out and clean up. Please accept the word of this prodigal. God can solve all the problems we have created in our marriages. Our Creator knows that as human beings living in a sinful world, we often fail Him. He is ready to forgive us and rescue us and our marriages from Satan.

Don't be discouraged if your divorce is about to be finalized, or even if it has already become final. Reconstruction of a marriage after a divorce has been granted is not uncommon unless we're listening to Satan's crowd. There is a reason that the Lord has you exactly where you are right now.

Consider the situation of the prodigal. This Jewish lad, prohibited by law from contact with swine, found himself literally living in a pig pen. If there was ever a family that had a right to give up on a prodigal because of situations and lifestyle, this man's family would have been the one. It is difficult for us living in modern times to imagine the shame and humiliation of the prodigal's family. Today they would be the talk of the town, or at least of the church. How could that family even think of his ever coming home? Perhaps Jesus gave this parable with that most extreme lifestyle illustration to show us that no matter how low the prodigal has sunk, his homecoming is still possible to the glory of God.

Although many prodigals change careers while in the far country, few actually take up feeding pigs for a living. Many prodigals do feed the pigs of alcoholism, drugs, and immorality. How could God expect anyone to wait with unconditional love for such a person to come home? Only when we are able to love and be loved as Christ did for us, can we then be ready to love our prodigals.

Perhaps you've read the references to the love of God and don't really understand how He loves us. If so, I have great news to share with you. News that can change not only your life, but your eternity.

The story is told of the farmer preparing for an approaching severe storm. As he prepared, he observed a flock of birds. Knowing they would be destroyed by the approaching weather, he opened the doors to his barn to provide a place of safety for them. Despite his good intentions, the birds didn't know of the danger they faced, nor that a place of safety had been provided. The farmer mused, "If I could become one of them for a little while, I could show them the way to safety."

In a much greater way, that's exactly what God did for mankind. Man by his nature is a sinner. We all fall short of being perfect. It may be possible for us to be good, but no one can live without sin. While it is true that many people attempt to lead good and moral lives, we all have sinned (Romans 3:23). Although God loves us, He hates our sin. Because of this, a provision was made by God for payment of our sin-debt.

Just as the farmer in the illustration desired to become one of the birds for a while to show them the way to safety, God Himself came to live on earth in the Person of Jesus Christ. Born of a virgin, Jesus lived a life without sin. He willingly died a cruel death on a cross to pay the price for my sins and yours. He arose from the grave on the third day and is alive today. When God looks at the life of one who has received His gift of eternal life, He does not see our sin, but the righteousness of Jesus Christ.

The Bible tells us that one day each person will stand before God and be judged. Our attempts to be good will be seen as filthy rags. They will not make us worthy to spend eternity with Him. However, the person who has received Jesus Christ as Savior will be recognized as spotless and worthy to dwell with Him for eternity.

Not only does God's Word, the Bible, promise life eternal to all who believe, it also promises us that God Himself will abide with us and be our Comforter throughout our lives. It is true that we are not promised a life without difficulty, but our Creator promises us that we will not be allowed to undergo more than we can bear.

How do we receive Christ and the gift of eternal life? By admitting that we are sinners and accepting the payment for our sins that Jesus Christ made by His death on the cross. Our sin debt is then transferred from us to Jesus Christ. Please don't wait until you polish up your act to receive Him, because it will never happen. Our God accepts us just as we are and where we are. He receives prodigals living in a pig pen as well as philanthropists living in penthouses. Our Heavenly Father waits for His children. God knows our hearts as we pray to receive Christ as our Savior.

If you are serious about getting right with God, you may wish to pray a prayer similar to this:

Dear God, I know that I am a sinner and cannot save myself. Right now I receive Jesus as my Savior and ask Him to forgive my sins. I invite Jesus into my life to be my Redeemer. Thank You, Father, for saving me. In Jesus' name I pray, Amen.

The Bible says that angels rejoice in Heaven when one person receives eternal life and becomes a child of His. If you have just prayed to receive Christ, I would encourage you to share this with another person before this day ends. You may wish to write or call the ministry. There's something about sharing your decision that affirms what has taken place (Romans 10:9-10).

You may also wish to open the Bible and let it speak to you as a new believer. The Gospel of John or First Thessalonians are excellent places to begin reading.

I've just asked you to consider the most important decision that can ever be made by man, a decision affecting your relationship with God and your eternal destiny. If you are still wavering, please take time to re-read this chapter. Ask God to show you His perfect plan for eternal life. Call a Christian friend or a pastor or our ministry and ask how you may be saved. Make plans now to attend a church on Sunday that holds the Bible as the infallible Word of God.

Were it necessary to condense this entire book into a single concept, it would be this: **Without Christ there is little real hope for a troubled marriage.**

At some time you will feel led to share with your spouse those words that make all the difference, "I am praying for you." Let me assure you that those five words brought tears to this prodigal's eyes more than once.

Perhaps you've stayed with me thus far and still are skeptical that your marriage can be restored. Yes, it can. The prodigal and spouse can be re-united by God with only one party standing for the marriage. The time may have come for you to make a commitment for your marriage.

Consider today declaring your intention to have a restored marriage, regardless of the present circumstances.

Does all this work? Does God really answer prayers for marriages? This prodigal is living proof that God answers prayers. I still can't explain why two years ago I drove one hundred miles on a hot July day, knocked on my wife's office window, and invited her to go to lunch with me. I can't explain why we obtained a marriage license without waiting. Nor can I explain why her pastor was available without notice to remarry us. I didn't plan to do any of these things. God, in His perfect timing, was answering the faithful prayers of a faithful wife.

Charlyne was a bit late returning from lunch that day, but even her employer rejoiced that her prodigal had come home.

PUTTING FAITH INTO ACTION -

The next time you're in the drugstore take a walk down the greeting card aisle and select a card for your spouse. Stay away from satire cards. I know you'll be surprised how many others jump out with just the right words. It doesn't have to say a lot just that you're thinking of your mate. You may even want to write a word of encouragement of your own before it is mailed. Perhaps by then you can write and say, "I am praying for you."

CHAPTER SIX

The Prodigal's Reasoning

"But when he came to himself, he said, 'How many of my father's hired servants have bread enough and to spare, and I perish with hunger!'" **Luke 15:17 (NKJV)**

During my time in the far country, the Lord took me to at least six different events where the parable of the prodigal son was dramatized. I never said that I learned my lessons from the Lord easily!

Although those dramas attempted to capture the emotion of the prodigal's decision to return home, it is impossible to act out what's taking place in the mind of the prodigal. The prodigal is being pulled in opposite directions. While perhaps he realizes God's will for his restored marriage, everything and everyone around him pressures him to "stay in the pig pen."

Most distressing to the mate, the prodigal appears to be weighing *returning home* against *staying in the far country*. For a period he may even attempt to live with one foot in each of those worlds.

One pull from the *far country* exceeds all others, however, and that is the prodigal's involvement with another person. Although this is a sensitive subject, it's one that needs to be discussed to fully understand the prodigal, his life in the *far country*, and the process of coming to the end of himself.

My dentist has a way of saying, "This might hurt a bit," and it usually does. As we look at this area of the prodigal's life, let me sound like my dentist. This may hurt a bit, but we'll benefit by understanding what is involved. I'm sorry to report that most prodigals become involved with another person, to some degree, while in the far country.

If you're the spouse waiting at home, please don't let the presence of another person discourage your waiting for your prodigal. There's good news for you in spite of the hurt. First, the other person fears the prayers of a spouse standing and praying for their marriage. There's no need to contact the other person to announce your intentions. They usually find out indirectly from the prodigal. Second, our Lord has a miraculous way of removing the other person in His timing, which is always at the right time.

One Sunday afternoon I received a call from my then divorced wife. After exchange of the usual pleasantries, she told me that she was praying for me to come home and knew that the Lord, at the right time, would restore our marriage. She then asked if I wanted to attend church with her that evening. I declined her invitation and quickly concluded the telephone call, somewhat amused at her thought that I would ever be coming home. My pig pen didn't smell bad enough yet for me to leave.

Later that evening, as I was walking into my church with my new girlfriend, half laughing, I told her about Charlyne's telephone call that afternoon. She actually stopped in her tracks in the middle of the street. She had already planted the vines that would someday cover our "happy cottage," and Charlyne had just poured the first big dose of weed killer on them. Months later, that other person told me she had known from that moment how things would end. I would be returning home.

Even after the presence of another person becomes known, continue to discount nearly all of what others and your prodigal are reporting about that person. More often than not, exactly the opposite is true. When your prodigal slips and reports that he has a friend and goes on to describe her as slender, rest assured she probably weighs more than you. Comments about cooking usually mean she can't boil water without burning it. Her children, reported to you as being well-behaved, are usually terrors. When you hear about his sudden attraction to domestic chores, remember that a new broom sweeps clean, especially when it's under a bit of pressure.

The spouse waiting at home should avoid asking questions about the other person. Your prodigal isn't likely to report that he was so lonely that he became involved with someone inferior to the wife he left, but often that is true. Another truth that you will not hear is that something (or many things) about that other person is reminding the prodigal of his own spouse. Let me illustrate. Charlyne's brother was killed while awaiting discharge from the Air Force. While in the far country, I was at a dinner party with my other person. A lady across the table was relating that her brother had been killed shortly before being discharged from the armed forces. I turned to my other person, whose brother was alive and well, and said, "That sounds like your brother."

The one waiting at home should never allow the prodigal to discuss intimate details. It's doubtful if you'll be hearing the truth, and Satan will take the facts you hear and attempt to discourage you in the days ahead.

Perhaps the most difficult assignment facing the praying spouse while waiting for the prodigal to return is knowing that another person is involved. If there were any way for you to avoid this hurt, I would waste no time sharing it with you. During the lonely times, let the love and grace of our Lord comfort you.

Let me run up a big red flag about the other person. Avoid Satan's ideas for you to become involved with someone to get back at the prodigal. God's plan for your marriage is only hindered when you let another person enter the picture. In the end, you'll cause the prodigal more concern by staying alone than by your becoming involved with another person.

Perhaps another red flag needs to go up to warn against attempting to make the prodigal jealous, even while the one at home is remaining true. The cause of Christ is never helped by such actions.

One spouse had a friend who dealt in classic cars. Arrangements were made for a strange car (usually a Corvette) to remain in the driveway all night and mysteriously disappear early the following morning. She also purchased a few items of men's clothing and hung them on her outside clothesline from time to time. It's not known if her prodigal ever saw her stage props. The only known result was a loss of her Christian testimony with her neighbors.

The spouse standing and praying for the prodigal's return needs to be on guard to avoid every appearance of an immoral lifestyle. Your prayers are causing Satan concern. Remember, he hates marriages, especially Christian marriages. He will take what you mean for good and make it look evil if it helps keep your family disrupted. It may sound old-fashioned, but even our prayer partners need to be the same sex. Avoid confiding in anyone of the opposite sex, except a professional counselor or your pastor. The next door neighbor might be a good listener, but the spouse at home is most vulnerable. It is important to avoid going out after church in a paired arrangement. No matter how innocent, Satan will take your good intentions and use it for evil.

An incident keeps coming to mind from my own time in the far country. Its inclusion here is only to illustrate to you how subtle Satan can be.

A year before our remarriage, Charlyne had taken vacation time to attend a week-long marriage conference out of state. By that time I knew (but could not accept) her unconditional love for me. She was praying and waiting for the day I would return home. At that time the medical office where she was administrator was searching for another physician. On the last day of her conference, the senior partner called to say they had been contacted by a physician a few miles away from where she was. He asked if Charlyne could meet the physician on her return trip.

That evening, after twelve hours of the conference, Charlyne drove a few hours in the opposite direction and checked into a hotel. She placed a call to the physician's answering service and received his return call. He was still making hospital rounds and had early office hours the next day. Charlyne's primary concern was to conclude her responsibility and start the sixteen hour drive home as early as possible. They agreed to meet at her hotel for a brief interview.

That same evening, thinking Charlyne to be on the way home, I called my children to see if they had heard from their mother. My youngest reported that Mom was staying another night and had gone to another city to meet a doctor. In his openness, he offered her hotel phone and room number. As Satan desired, I called her during the five-minute period the Christian physician had come by her room for his brief interview. Today she and I laugh at Satan's timing and his attempt to ruin for us all she had learned that week.

The Bible tells us that God will not be mocked. There is a price to pay for sin, and there is a reward for doing His will. Having been a prodigal, I understand the hurt, the confusion, and the frustration that affect everyone when someone leaves for the far country.

When life becomes difficult because of another person, go to God in prayer, seeking His guidance and comfort. Pray for your own family as well as for the other person. There's a good possibility that your other person is someone else's prodigal.

PUTTING FAITH INTO ACTION -

While waiting for your prodigal, try spending some time renewing your bedroom. While staying within the budget, your efforts can go from rearranging and cleaning to a complete redecoration. Your prodigal will come home a different person. In your spare time prepare a new bedroom to welcome him home. If the present bedroom reminds you of some bad times, those memories might be eased after you become creative.

CHAPTER SEVEN

The Wise Prodigal

"'I will arise and go to my father, and will say to him, "Father, I have sinned against heaven and before you,"'
Luke 15:18 (NKJV)

Although not intentional, much of what has been said thus far seems to have been directed at the female waiting at home for her male prodigal. While this is often the case, there are also many men waiting for their prodigal wives.

Charlyne reports that some of the most godly men she has known were those attending a support group for spouses standing for their marriages. After their mates left, these people chose not to alter their course, but to declare their purpose; praying and standing for their prodigal's return.

While living in the far country, I met and spoke with prodigals of both sexes. Every concept expressed in the preceding chapters could apply equally to both male and female prodigals. Please don't discontinue reading because there is a male pronoun where your situation should have a female pronoun, or vice versa. An entire book of he/she references would make rather dull reading.

God has a great way of somehow allowing prodigals to review the material the spouse is using to help pray him home. Despite the prodigal's excuses (I have a friend who needs to read that), most review, to some extent, anything passed along from home. Strange as it may seem, the prodigal's other person often reads this material as well. While this may be done under the pretense of knowing the enemy, our God may use this to help remove the other person from your prodigal's life. The other person who has read thus far would perhaps by now be giving some thought to folding up the tent and moving on. There's no long-term future with a prodigal when a spouse is praying and standing for the marriage.

If you're a prodigal, please allow me to say from the bottom of my heart that I understand your situation and feelings. While life may be difficult for many reasons, it is not hopeless. In fact, there is more hope for you than can be imagined.

A young boy was home alone with his dad on a Saturday afternoon. The dad was attempting to watch a football game, and his bored son, was constantly interrupting. Seeking enough silence to finish the game, the father ripped a page from a magazine lying next to his chair. He then tore the page, a map of the world, into dozens of small pieces. "Here," he said, giving the handful of torn paper to his son, "put the puzzle together for me."

Within minutes, junior returned with the map carefully taped back together. Observing the almost impossible task completed, his dad asked the son how he completed the puzzle so quickly. "It was easy," the son explained. "On the back of the map was a picture of Jesus. After I saw Jesus the right way, the world was right."

During my time in the far country, I had the process backward. I was trying to make my world look right without any real success. Each time I would solve a piece of the puzzle of my life, two others would be out of place. Had I looked at my Lord first, my world with my wife would have looked right to me.

My prodigal friend, don't give up. God had a reason and purpose for allowing you and your spouse to meet and to be joined together in marriage, becoming one flesh. No matter how bleak your world appears, you may well be closer to solving the puzzle of your life than you can imagine. Please don't play the *what if* game over your marriage situation. Those who study human behavior tell us that ninety-seven percent of *what ifs* that cross our mind never happen, and that we have little or no control over the other three percent. I feel that Satan used *what ifs* more than anything else to hinder God's plan for the restoration of my marriage.

Each time a *what if* thought crosses your mind, it might be helpful to turn it into a positive thought immediately. One of my most common *what ifs* dealt with the possibility of losing my job. *"What if* I go home and then lose my job?" My wife will have no respect for me as a man. That could have been turned into, *"What if* I go home and then get a better job?" My wife will be proud of me. My regret is that I didn't adopt this thought process early on during my prodigal days but walked in fear of possible rejection.

By the way, the specific *what if* that I worried about so much actually happened. Several months after our remarriage, the company where I was employed eliminated my position, and I was terminated. Months of playing *what if* didn't stop the process. But there's good news. My termination (all right, I was fired) allowed me the opportunity to fulfill a lifelong dream.

My son, Tim, and I are now partners in a family business. As with any new business there are some difficult times, but these are far outweighed by the privilege and joy of working with my first-born son every day. My old prodigal eyes that had seen much of the far country were not dry the evening our family joined hands with our pastor and a few close friends in our living room. There we dedicated our small business to God as a ministry for Him. Had I remained in the far country, I still would have lost my job.

Instead of working with Tim, I would be employed somewhere else, but still suffering from a broken relationship with my family, including Tim. Not only did my *if* worries fail to prevent my job loss, there is no way with my own efforts that I could have arranged for our business to be established. If only someone had told me to stop trying and start trusting God, my days in the pig pen would have been shortened.

The wise prodigal is the one who recognizes that God has a special claim on his life and his marriage. He observes the unconditional love of a spouse standing for their marriage and realizes the spouse is demonstrating love that goes beyond human reasoning. The wise prodigal probably isn't able to do all that our Lord would have him do immediately, but he becomes increasingly aware of God's guidance in his life.

Years ago our daughter, Lori, had an older model car that she used for transportation to school. Although safe, it was so old that she usually didn't drive it farther than about ten miles from home. One particular day, I recall that this old car wouldn't start. We managed to push it to the service station where the family purchases gas. The logo and sign out front indicated they offered mechanical services. The man I spoke with appeared to be a mechanic. He seemed to have all the tools. He had mechanic-looking hands and even provided a couple of guesses on why the car wouldn't run. Repairs were made, and Lori picked her car up the following day. She had driven less than a mile when the problem recurred. Again, I pushed her back to our mechanic friend. That afternoon the car was picked up and, once again, quit running a few blocks from the station. After five trips to the mechanic we took the car to an automobile dealer. The gas station man who appeared to be a mechanic had actually caused some additional problems in his attempts to correct the original one.

Reflecting upon my life experiences, I can recall times when I cared for my marriage much like I did Lori's car. There always seemed to be someone or something around who claimed to be a mechanic for marriages. Looking for inexpensive solutions in the wrong places ended up costing me my marriage for a time. Many of us have attempted marriage repairs by the mechanic of money. If only we had a few more dollars, we reason, things would be different. When that doesn't work, we push our disabled marriage to the mechanic of a new home. When the marriage stalls out again, we try the mechanic of more leisure time. Some even opt for the mechanic of an outside relationship.

After Lori's fifth attempt to have her car repaired, she was ill-advised by that unknowing mechanic that the vehicle wasn't worth fixing and that she should get a new one. The most dangerous mechanic for a troubled marriage is the one who advises us that our problems are too great to ever be resolved; that there's no hope trying to fix up our broken families. Despite that mechanic's advice, the concept of a second marriage – a different marriage – doesn't work.

Lori's car was quite a sight when I saw it in the dealer's service area. Unidentified parts from the engine were lying in the back seat. A multiplicity of wires hung from under the dash. The entire steering column had been removed. "No problem," the dealer assured me. "You just have to know how it's made to be able to repair it properly."

Who is the wise prodigal? He is the one who avoids the marriage mechanics of this world and presents a hopeless marriage to the Creator of life, our Lord Jesus, for His healing touch. Regardless of whether you're a prodigal or the one standing for the marriage, the One who created you in His image is waiting for you to allow Him to work His miracle in your marriage.

The following poem written in 1988 says it all:

Restore Our Marriage

To us it is no secret, what the Lord wants to do.
Restore our marriage and make us happy, too.
What He's done for millions, He's wanting to do,
Restore our marriage, make our family new.

We have our doubts, think it can't be done,
When we trust in Jesus, He'll make us the one.
It matters not how bad the past has been
Let the blood of Jesus cover all your sin.

Others will say divorce is the thing to do.
Even a court may say the marriage is through,
Our Lord is wanting His perfect will to do,
Restore our marriage, make our family new.

To us it is no secret, what the Lord wants to do,
Restore our marriage and make us happy too.
What He's done for millions, He's wanting to do,
Restore our marriage, make our family new.

PUTTING FAITH INTO ACTION -

Some of my most encouraging times in the far country took place while walking. We often surround ourselves with television, radio, and other distractions while at home. Although the physicians could cite several physical benefits, going for a walk often allows an emotional renewing. Perhaps the cheapest and most refreshing vacation that can be taken is around your own block. Plan to take a long walk, allowing time to listen to yourself and to your Lord. You'll appreciate the results so much that you may wish to start walking on a regular basis.

CHAPTER EIGHT

The Unworthy Prodigal

"'And I am no longer worthy to be called your son. Make me like one of your hired servants.'" **Luke 15:19 (NKJV)**

One of the most significant events since our remarriage to each other took place rather spontaneously on a Sunday morning. I had the opportunity to stand and thank our church family for having prayed for our family and for our marriage to be restored. The first Sunday after we were remarried, I returned to the church Charlyne attended and where we had previously been active as a family for several years. Although our marriage had not been officially announced, several people offered congratulations. Many gave reports of their having prayed for us.

As we were singing a congregational hymn, I began to think about the people who had been praying for what some considered a lost cause, a divorced family. These people had heartaches and problems more than enough for themselves without having been concerned about our recent marriage.

One lady had cared for an invalid husband for several years before he went to be with Jesus. Now she cared for her sister who was in poor health. Despite financial pressures, there was always a smile on her face. She always found time to help out whenever needed at her church. She's one of those people I described earlier whose prayers caused things to happen. Privately, before the service began, she confided that she had prayed for me every morning for more than two years.

The theme of that particular service dealt with the family of God. The pastor gave an opportunity for testimonies from the congregation. Before the "physical Bob" could stop the "spiritual Bob," I stood and began to speak, thanking the church for the prayers from which I couldn't run. Today I can't recall a single word spoken. I do know that on that Sunday morning, I made my peace with my church family.

Had anyone suggested to me a year earlier that I would be in that particular church, remarried and giving a testimony, I would have probably laughed. Had anyone told me a year earlier that people who had the heart of God in their devotional life were praying for me to come home, I would have been moved. Even though I had traveled to the far country and was living in a pig pen, I still realized that when people who were right with God prayed, things happened!

One of the most destructive weapons of the enemy is his ability to convince the prodigal of his own unworthiness. The prodigal reasons that because of having gone to the far country and having attempted to make a new life in a pig pen, God couldn't possibly love him anymore. And even if God could (according to Satan's reasoning), how could a prodigal expect his former spouse to ever love him again? The answer lies in the fact that only part of that reasoning is accurate. God couldn't possibly love the prodigal any more than He does. His love is so great He gave His only Son, Jesus, to die and pay the penalty for the prodigal's sin.

It still amazes me that while I felt unworthy to consider coming home to my wife and serving God in our family's church, I could attend another church with a girlfriend at my side and consider myself worthy of God's best for me in the new life that I envisioned.

It would be difficult for me to imagine the number of people on whom our divorce had destructive effects. Even though Charlyne and I led rather quiet lives, the decision to abandon our marriage impacted our children, parents, grandparents, church friends, co-workers, distant relatives, and countless others. In addition to the direct results of the heartaches we caused those close to us, the indirect results that our having given up what seemed to most to be a rather normal marriage, often becomes Satan's stamp of approval for others to end their marriages.

If there was ever one to feel unworthy of God's love it should have been me. It's not necessary to go into detail for you to understand that my life in the far country was, indeed, wasted with riotous living. Attempting to mask the guilt of having left my family, I tried life in every corner of the pig pen and found only more pigs and guilt. Nothing compounds feelings of unworthiness more than observing the Christ-like lifestyle being led by a spouse standing and praying for the prodigal's return.

Perhaps there's a skeptical spouse considering her prodigal's return but feeling that her prodigal is different. Even though she desires his return, life in his far country has been so extreme that he will never again be worthy of her love. The memories of the past days will always be too much to ever again allow them to love each other.

When God created us, He knew exactly how we would fail Him. Despite our failures and rejection of His love, God continues to love each of us with His unconditional love. That love continues in spite of circumstances and in spite of our rejection of Him. It is necessary that we develop a similar love for our spouse so that we can love in spite of lifestyle, and often even in spite of rejection. Unconditional love combined with prayer goes far toward setting the stage for the return of your prodigal.

Our God has created us so that our memory tends to accent positive events and to forget negative events with the passing of time. This is good news to anyone standing for their marriage. While a prodigal, I could easily recall many happy times of marriage and family life. I began to have difficulty focusing on the negative events that had taken place.

This same concept is good news for the marriage after the prodigal returns. Memories of my own time in the far country continue to diminish. After all, there aren't many good memories of life in a pig pen. Please don't fail to stand for your marriage because of the memories you fear the prodigal will bring home. Allow the Holy Spirit of God to do His work on the memories of both spouses.

Another subtle trick of Satan is to attempt to convince the spouse who is standing for her marriage of her own unworthiness. Remember that God created you and your spouse for each other. Please allow your Creator to remind you daily that you are worthy for your life mate. Our Lord is ready to help you when thought patterns might make you feel unworthy.

Please don't allow yourself to feel unworthy because of the comments of others. Charlyne heard frequently that standing and praying for her marriage was an easy way out; an escape from having to deal with the trauma of divorce. Nothing could be further from the truth. **Making a commitment to stand for a marriage is declaring spiritual warfare against Satan.** If your spouse has left (or is about to leave home), Satan thinks he has won the battle in your home. The worthy individual is the one who takes a stand for what is known to be right in the sight of God.

When Satan is unable to defeat you, he will attempt to defeat someone whose defeat will defeat you. Although not very good sentence structure, perhaps the concept can be seen. The spouse proves her worthiness by standing for the marriage. It won't be long before you hear of someone who has divorced, perhaps with less reason than you have. Resist at all cost the urge to look around at what others are doing. Look up to Christ for your example.

Perhaps our Lord will use a different event than a testimony in church on a Sunday morning, but it will happen. Something in the future will affirm to you and your spouse that you are both worthy of God's love. Then you can experience the joy of being worthy of each other as well. This prodigal can testify that day is worth all the waiting and praying that is involved.

PUTTING FAITH INTO ACTION -

During times of marriage problems most of us tend to become somewhat self-centered. We spend all our energy and most of our time being concerned about our own situation. Instead do something for another person with no possibility of repayment. Bake a pie for the widower next door. Send a note of encouragement to a shut-in. Help the elderly man down the block with his shopping. I can promise that you'll both feel better because of your efforts.

CHAPTER NINE

The Prodigal's Family

"And he arose and came to his father. But when he was still a great way off, his father saw him and had compassion, and ran and fell on his neck and kissed him."
Luke 15:20 (NKJV)

It is interesting to note that no record is given of the prodigal's father going to the far country seeking his prodigal. Not until the prodigal made a personal decision to return home and had actually started his journey did the father take any physical action to bring the wanderer home.

Without question, the most difficult decisions associated with standing and praying for a prodigal spouse to return home deal with what actions should or should not be undertaken. The good news is that the Holy Spirit of God will direct each decision we face, when we allow Him to work in our lives. God will affirm to you, according to His will for your life, when the time is right. For example, ask your spouse to come for dinner. Any more suggestions from me on specific issues might hinder God's working in your marriage. What may be pleasing to God for one couple might not be in His will for another.

Waiting is not one of my strong points. I've always been early for appointments and feel everyone else should be as well. When a business call takes me across the state, I can usually predict within minutes my return time. In one way, I'm thankful that Charlyne was the one originally waiting on God's will to be done in our marriage. Had I been the one waiting at home, my patience would have undergone quite a test during that time.

Some time ago I heard one of those sermons which demand that notes be taken. The minister was presenting good Bible-based material faster than I could comprehend. In fact, he was preaching faster than I could even take notes, so I began to abbreviate. Later I discovered I had used the same abbreviation for two terms in that sermon. I had penned W.O.G. for will of God as well as for waiting on God. Looking at my notes, I realized the two terms were somewhat interchangeable. Our Lord brings special comfort to the prodigal's family in matters regarding W.O.G.

Prior to the birth of our first child, it seemed nine months was going to be too long to wait. My impatient nature wanted our son much quicker. Although some babies are born much sooner and do well, strong and healthy babies are usually full-term. Just as I would not have wanted to hasten our son's birthing process, we cannot hasten God's return process for the prodigal. Each day our child remained in his mother's womb he became stronger. Likewise, each day the prodigal remains in the far country, someone is being strengthened. Perhaps it's even you.

While staying carefully away from specifics, there are some general concepts regarding actions that may be helpful to the spouse waiting for a prodigal's return. Along with the positive actions, there needs to be some admonition against possible destructive actions as well. As much as I dislike the little word *don't*, let's get those out of the way before looking at the positive actions. The positives are much more enjoyable.

We could sum up all the *don'ts* with one general statement: Don't burn any bridges behind you. Regardless of how much you are hurting, talk to God (only) about your negative plans before carrying them out. The prodigal's trip, although still possible, will be more difficult if he's having to cross burned bridges to return home.

Avoid burning bridges by your physical actions. For example:

Don't cause him to lose his job.

Don't attempt to ruin his credit.

Don't burn clothing he left behind.

Don't confront his other person.

Don't sink his fishing boat.

Don't have his new telephone tapped.

Don't have him arrested.

Don't approach his new neighbors.

Don't stake out his apartment.

Don't cut his tires.

Don't damage personal items left at home.

Don't put glue in his door locks.

Don't have his dog put to sleep.

Don't place his obituary in the newspaper.

Avoid burning bridges by your words. For example:

Don't tell others that he has lost his mind.

Don't discredit him to his parents.

Don't discredit him to your children.

Don't discuss details of his lifestyle in the far country.

Don't gossip at church about your divorce.

Don't tell others he may be homosexual.

Don't rumor that he may have a social disease.

These examples may sound like extremes, but they really aren't. I have known the people involved in each incident I just shared. Fortunately, all these events didn't happen to the same person.

Unloading a rumor about your prodigal may make you feel somewhat justified, temporarily. However, the person who hears the rumor, as well as those who hear the later amplified versions, will remember the same material after your prodigal returns. Don't give someone an opportunity to look at you and your mate after the marriage is restored and wonder, "Why did she want him back if he..." The cause of Christ and other marriages will be damaged. If a guideline is needed, try not to say anything about your prodigal unless it could be said from the pulpit of your church. Although that may hinder your talk, it will help your marriage.

We've come this far without using the "A" word, but our consideration of separation and divorce wouldn't be complete without discussing attorneys. First let me say that some of the godliest people I know are Christian attorneys. They have a daily walk with Jesus that is an example to others. Should the time come in your marriage situation that you need to consult an attorney, please seek out a godly attorney to represent you. Before an attorney is retained, ask his stand on marriage reconciliation. If he turns a deaf ear to God's provision for one man and one woman for a lifetime, find another attorney immediately.

Some of the greatest devastation to impact a marriage comes from receiving inappropriate legal advice. Perhaps it's been a few months since the separation. Although your prodigal has filed for divorce, you and he are still able to communicate. You may find talking with him now more exciting than when he was living at home. He's usually available when a crisis happens. He will not have recognized that God has started doing His work in your failing marriage.

Because of the pending divorce, you have been advised to retain an attorney. Early on, your new attorney advises you to stop communicating "in any way" with your spouse. You are told that your attorney and his attorney will do all the negotiating that is necessary. Although that advice doesn't settle well with you, you agree because it's an attorney's advice. A short time later, something you say to your attorney is misrepresented to your spouse by his attorney and a legal battle is underway. The work our God desired to do in your marriage just struck a human obstacle.

If you need an attorney, ask God to lead you to one who can help, not hinder, the Lord's plans. A good starting place in that search might be to ask others who are standing for their marriages and can report positive experiences with specific attorneys.

I feel that one of the first positive factors in our journey to remarriage was Charlyne's having retained a godly attorney prior to our divorce. At no point did he place any undue pressure on her for anything. We were allowed to work out our own property settlement agreement. He sent the necessary court notices by regular mail so I wouldn't have to miss work to accept certified mail.

A word of caution. Please don't feel that just because an attorney attends your church, he will be supportive of your standing for the marriage. Unfortunately, some people in every profession (including my own funeral director peers) become active in a church to make business contacts. Many people claim to be Christians, but they have never truly made Jesus Lord, nor do they walk the walk of a Christian. A brief conversation will reveal the professional's true motives.

Charlyne had consulted two other attorneys prior to selecting a third to assist her. The first two maintained excellent reputations in very large local churches. Attorney number one had been a friend of our family for many years. Although he refused to help her obtain a divorce, feeling it to be wrong, he spent time tracking me down in the far country to see how he might help us restore our marriage without going through with the divorce. Unfortunately, when this happened I hadn't yet reached the lowest part of the pig pen and wasn't ready for anyone's help. Fortunately, I couldn't stop his prayers from reaching Heaven. A bill was never received for Charlyne's consultation with him.

Attorney number two had a reputation for helping Christian couples during divorce. During Charlyne's initial visit, she was told how much he could get from me, although I had little for him to go after. When questioned, my wife was advised that he would have been willing to go after either of us and that she was fortunate to have an opportunity to retain his services before I called on him. She was also given the "don't communicate with your husband" rule. Charlyne paid for her consultation and left that office.

Attorney number three was the godly man who, although allowing us to divorce, prayed for our marriage and permitted my wife and I to make our own decisions during the process. He went out of his way to help rather than hinder the early working of God's Holy Spirit on our failed marriage.

Attorneys who are committed to stopping a divorce have a special ministry. If you need legal counsel, ask your prayer partners to pray for God to lead you to the individual our God has waiting to help.

Do I need an attorney? Should I contest the divorce? Should I ask for alimony? These and similar questions can't be given blanket answers. God's Holy Spirit will guide you and provide answers to each question as you stand for your marriage and seek to carry out His will for your life.

Should our God allow your marriage to reach the stage of a final divorce, there's no reason to give up praying and standing. Had Charlyne given up when a judge said we were divorced, I would still be in the far country and living in a pig pen today. I thank God from the bottom of my being that my wife's love was unconditional.

Several months ago I read a newspaper article about a family from my hometown in Kentucky. Their story was so unusual that it had been picked up by a news wire service. This Christian couple had been divorced. The wife stood and prayed for their marriage. When God brought her prodigal home they didn't remarry, they went to court and had their divorce annulled. Their story radiated the love and hope that Christ Jesus can provide when Satan attempts to ruin a marriage. Articles like that can cause prodigals to do a lot of thinking.

Someday I hope to meet that couple. I imagine they will agree that all their family's hurt during the separation and divorce was worth the price. That national news story probably caused many prodigals to count the high cost of running from the love their God and their spouse hold for them. *"Therefore what God has joined together, let man not separate." Mark 10:9*

PUTTING FAITH INTO ACTION -

Although it may not be realized, your standing for a marriage and faithful attendance at church is a source of encouragement to your pastor. The one who remains true to God while in the valley stands out to a pastor even though sitting in church alone. You probably come to his mind often during his time with God. Please make a special effort to encourage your pastor during this time. Depending on your relationship to the parsonage family, do something to encourage your encourager. Even though a home-baked apple pie and a note would be welcomed, a small greeting card would mean just as much.

CHAPTER TEN

A Worthy Welcome

"And the son said to him, 'Father, I have sinned against heaven and in your sight, and am no longer worthy to be called your son.' But the father said to his servants, 'Bring out the best robe and put it on him, and put a ring on his hand and sandals on his feet.'" **Luke 15:21-22 (NKJV)**

Regardless of the circumstances, there is probably no greater joy on earth than receiving praise when condemnation is deserved and anticipated. The prodigal returning home didn't even have shoes for his feet. Yet he was received in royal fashion.

Were that parable to take place today, consider the consequences. The son had wasted a fortune, disgraced his family, led an ungodly lifestyle, and was now returning to his family. Most of us functioning under human reasoning would have turned him away.

We need to remember Jesus' purpose for having given this parable. He was attempting to illustrate the unconditional love that the Heavenly Father has for each of His children. Before coming to Christ, each of us, no matter how good and moral, lived as a prodigal before God. Lives and fortunes were wasted. We had unconfessed sin and turned our backs on the love of our Heavenly Father.

The individual who can't understand how a spouse can be waiting with unconditional love for a prodigal seems to be saying they can't understand the love that our God had for them before they came to Christ.

Unfortunately, it is often the people who need to be most supportive of the standing and praying spouse who are the first to challenge why anyone would want a prodigal back.

Perhaps parents have the most difficult time understanding how their adult child, having been hurt by a mate, could ever consider taking that person back. We all seek approval from parents, regardless of our age, in life's decisions. During a time of separation and divorce, the greatest gift that parents can give an adult child isn't financial support. It is the gift of understanding and support for their child who has taken the difficult path of standing for a marriage according to God's standards. Unfortunately, many well-intentioned parents reverse the process, offering financial assistance that allows their child to divorce the prodigal.

It is even more regrettable that often Christian parents have the most difficulty comprehending unconditional love for a prodigal. The proudest parents in this world should be those who, although a divorce is taking place in the life of one of their children, realize they brought up a child who recognizes God's biblical principle of *one man and one woman for one's lifetime* and is standing for that principle in his life, believing God for reconciliation to occur.

Within thirty minutes of our home there are thousands of people who are separated or who have divorced. As I write this chapter, it is 4 A.M. on a Saturday. Many of those lonely people are now making their way out of the bars, possibly taking home a stranger just to avoid being alone for a few hours. Tonight the process will start all over again. These people are seeking the solution to divorce in pills, bottles, and sex. The best they can anticipate is finding a person who will marry them and end the cycle, at least for a while. God's claim on their lives is being ignored.

There's also another large group in our community who, in spite of separation or divorce, are leading godly lives as they wait for His timing to bring their spouses home. They have chosen not to live the sinful lifestyle that society seems to encourage following divorce. Their decision is to remain alone with God, praying and standing for their one flesh mate to make his peace with God and then return home to the family.

Parents, if your adult child is going through a divorce and has chosen to stand for their marriage, no doubt you are hurting, and you may feel you have failed as a parent. Regardless, you should thank God every day that someone made a decision to save the marriage. If it were me, I would feel a thousand times better knowing my daughter or son went to bed talking with our God and will get up today to serve Him instead of having spent the past few hours in a bar seeking temporal relief in earthly ways. Although the heartache is still there, each of us who have read the Bible, know how the story will end.

By the way, there's no greater source of encouragement to an adult child standing for a marriage than for parents to acknowledge their support and prayers for that marriage. This may require you to admit that you were wrong in the past and to ask your adult child's forgiveness. God will honor and bless your decision to support that broken marriage. If you've been withholding a few "rings and robes," because someone is standing, this might be a good time to bring them out. Your support will encourage your child.

How is the parable of the prodigal and marriage alike? They are both about the restoration of relationships of undeserving people. The parents and in-laws who can offer unconditional love to both prodigal and spouse do much to allow God to restore that marriage.

If you're standing for your marriage against the well-meaning advice of your parents, please don't become discouraged. Your decision to wait for the life mate God has given you, speaks more to them of your faith than volumes of books on the love of God. On that day when you and your spouse are reunited, you'll see their true feelings. The impact of your restored marriage on the lives of others, including parents, will be like dropping a pebble into still water. The ripples will reach places we can't even imagine.

We've come this far with only one brief mention regarding those on whom your decision to stand (or not to stand) for your marriage will have the greatest effect, your children. I am grateful that children and divorce are today being openly discussed, even by the secular media. Both secular and Christian writers will advise you that children do not get over divorce regardless of their age at the time of the trauma. We need to prepare early on to help our children give a worthy welcome to their prodigal parent. It is extremely difficult for a child to watch a parent leave home, hear the remaining parent discredit the one who left, and then, sometime later have the absent parent return and expect their love and acceptance.

In another home, the children watch as the parent prepares for a date, seeking that new someone who will make life perfect. These children know they will be left with a babysitter or alone, depending on age, for the evening. Later that night, when they're supposed to be asleep, they hear the parent returning. Already awake, they overhear goodbyes that take too long inside the front door. Frequently the parent participates in dating behavior that is not tolerated for teenagers in the same home.

It doesn't take a master's degree in psychology to determine which home is better serving the interests of the children. Standing for a marriage teaches our children that no problem is too big for our God. Even very young children can understand that concept. Another red flag, avoid at all cost discrediting the prodigal to the children. It is possible to include your children while praying for a parent to return, without having to share all you know. If there is no meat for dinner tonight, don't tell the children that *dad spent all his money this past weekend when he went away with the redhead from work and couldn't make the child support payment for his family.* **Tell God the details and your children the need.**

Don't become too alarmed if your children tell you that they don't want the prodigal spouse to ever return. It's possible to love your mate as if nothing had happened. Proper actions on the part of the standing spouse will allow children of that marriage to participate in one of the greatest object lessons in faith that can be given.

When standing for your marriage, please don't feel that your children will be harmed by your stand. No matter how difficult or how young the children, they will be able to see biblical faith as you pray. Your dependence on the Lord for every need can be displayed daily in your own home.

Weigh carefully the options for your children. The person deciding to allow Satan to have the marriage and desiring to build a new life will expect the children, at some point, to shift emotions from the absent parent to a new substitute parent. At the most insecure time in their lives, the children are placed in competition with another person for a parent's attention. No matter how well the new person seems to get along with your children, there is no replacement for the absent parent.

In one home we know of, the standing parent is including her older children in prayer for family restoration. She and her children pray for their material needs to be met, and they are confident that God, who has brought them this far, will not let them down. Together they pray for their prodigal to not only come home, but for his safety while he is away.

One more red flag. Both parents need to avoid using their children as pawns in the game of life. Their young worlds are already upside down. Don't place them in the middle by demanding they take sides between the two of you. Besides, there are usually three sides, his, hers, and the truth. Both spouses need to reach agreement in their dealing with the children. While it may take a court to determine that the children see dad on alternate weekends and must be home by 5:30 P.M. on Sunday, it takes two parents in agreement about the welfare of their children to determine what will happen and what will be discussed (or not discussed) during that weekend.

The separated or divorced parents who can agree on this one matter have gone far toward protecting their children from some of the pains of divorce. The discussion of children and divorce could continue for a few hundred pages. As in other matters, when you are standing for your marriage and living daily with Jesus at your side, He will give you direction in everything, especially matters regarding your precious children.

Please don't become discouraged when you leave Jesus behind and take over for a while in matters relating to the children. Although we would each like to respond perfectly to every situation as He would direct, we're living in an imperfect world and undergoing some real trials of our faith. When God created us, He knew exactly how we would fail Him.

As soon as you realize you've pulled your children away from Jesus, immediately return them to Him and seek His forgiveness. Secondly, seek to restore a right attitude with your children.

Monday evening at dinner, junior pushes his plate of beans away, demanding meat for dinner like all his friends have in their homes. Your day has been trying, even before junior's mini-hunger strike. Without thinking, you unload all the garbage about no child support, the mate's weekend with the red head from the office, throwing in a few more suspicions for good measure. A few minutes later, junior is sulking to his room leaving you alone to stare at his uneaten plate of beans. No, you haven't blown it yet.

The next steps determine if our God gains the victory. Going to your own room, feeling a failure, questioning why you're even trying, and having a pity party about what a mess your life has become gives the victory of that battle to Satan. Confessing to God that you've failed again and then asking junior to forgive you for all that was said gives our Lord the victory. Losing a few battles with the enemy of marriage doesn't mean we're going to lose the war.

By the way, how did that evening end? After your talk with junior and a few hugs, he wandered out, ate his beans, and then even cleaned and washed his own plate for you. Our God always affirms when we're living His way.

PUTTING FAITH INTO ACTION -

At an appropriate time, write either a card or letter to parents involved on both sides of your marriage. Express your unconditional love for them and for your mate without sounding like a sermon. Allow them to see the precious person that is waiting for the prodigal.

CHAPTER ELEVEN

Preparing For The Prodigal's Return

"'And bring the fatted calf here and kill it, and let us eat and be merry;'" **Luke 15:23 (NKJV)**

Our local church will be starting revival services in a few days. We have been encouraged by our pastor to prepare for these special services. Other conflicting meetings on the church calendar have been postponed. Flyers have been printed and distributed. By now, ushers have been arranged for each evening and housing accommodations made for the visiting evangelist. Although these items are important, that's not the preparation our pastor has been encouraging us to make. He's speaking of a deeper preparation that which takes place in each of our lives.

As we prepare for the return of a prodigal spouse, we must look carefully at our preparations. When I returned from the far country, I appreciated my part of the closet having been emptied, as well as a recently redecorated bedroom. Although I came home to these nice touches, I didn't come home because of these things.

While it may be helpful and encouraging for you to spend time on the physical part of the anticipated return, the real preparation needs to be spiritual. When should it begin? As soon as you have taken a stand for your marriage and begun believing God for the return home of your prodigal spouse.

In the parable, the prodigal didn't return home for the best robe, the ring, and the shoes. Had that been his motivation, he would probably have gathered these additional valuable items and departed again for the far country. He received these gifts from the father because he came home, not so that he would come home.

In the parable, the father placed these items on his son with an unconditional love. He didn't bring out the robe, have his son try it on, and then promise that priceless garment to him after he had proven himself worthy of such a gift. He didn't show the sparkle of the ring in the sunlight and then put it away. Nor were the shoes withheld until those feet, still filthy from the pig pen, were cleaned up a bit.

In a symbolic way, it is possible for you to bring forth the best robe and put it on your prodigal, place a ring on his hand, and shoes on his feet, even before your prodigal arrives home. Once you have placed symbolic garments on your prodigal, they are not to be removed for any reason. That best robe we can wrap around a prodigal spouse is the robe of prayer. In addition to hiding the prodigal's flaws, it can comfort and protect him.

Constant communication with God in prayer and Bible reading make it necessary at some point for the spouse standing for the marriage to examine and correct their own personal spiritual flaws. If this entire book had to be condensed, the one concept that would have to remain is: **only God can restore your marriage**.

Even though your prodigal continues to display no outward evidence of a desire to come home from the far country, your walk with Christ must be constant. Your obedience to continue "having done all – to stand" is one key to a restored marriage. Many outstanding books and CDs designed to take the seeking individual into a closer relationship with Christ are available. My efforts to provide step by step instruction to you would fall far short of the spiritual counsel available from others.

Although it's no excuse, remember that I was the prodigal while my wife was standing for our marriage. She had to learn how to live her life totally dependent on our Lord Jesus Christ. I can, however, testify that the spiritual life of a prodigal begins to be affected, although perhaps unnoticed by others, as soon as the spouse declares her purpose for the marriage and becomes serious about the Christian life.

While I have stayed carefully away from providing a complete devotional and prayer guide for those praying for a marriage, I can share some of the concepts that my wife used when standing. Without a doubt, **the starting place for prayer needs to be forgiveness.** Because of what has taken place to the family, some spouses tend to stumble for a while right there on the starting block. Until the prodigal can be forgiven, past, present, and future, the standing spouse cannot attempt to bring him in from the far country. Communication with God is blocked. Please don't allow Satan to slip in a couple *but he's*...on your prayer life. Recognize where the negative thoughts are coming from.

Charlyne used two favorite prayer guides. One was a detailed expansion of praying *The Lord's Prayer* on a daily basis. The second, and one of my favorites, included printed prayers, with space for inclusion of specific names. Such prayers were included for the spouse, their children; the spouse's other person, and several other people. These were also given to her prayer partners. I was greatly moved the first time I saw the prayers that my one flesh wife, as well as several others, were praying for our marriage each day.

Please don't feel that I'm dropping the most important subject in this book at this point. God has prepared a special plan for you to learn to walk with Christ and then to pray your spouse home. I feel very uncomfortable making any attempt to provide specific *how to's* in prayer matters. You will find that Rejoice Marriage Ministries, Christian book stores, and possibly your church library have many books and devotional guides that the Lord can use to help you during these current days of crisis. They will also benefit you for the rest of your life. Some of the best material for personal devotions to use during times of divorce and separation can be obtained from one of the groups of people standing for their marriages.

Only when the standing spouse declares a compete abandonment of human plans and schemes to bring the prodigal home, is God's power able to be effective. Why keep trying when you can be trusting?

The vehicle I drive is a white mini-van. Like most men, I have something of a love relationship with my vehicle. Had Charlyne come to the far country and attempted with her own power to push my van toward home, she probably would not have moved it the first inch. Although the van has the power sufficient to take it where it needs to go, pushing by hand is not very effective. Had Charlyne called on the manufacturer and then read the instruction book, she could have easily started the engine and had the van driven home. Her continuing attempts to push when power was available would have been foolish. Likewise, we are foolish if we are trying to push prodigal spouses home when we can call on the One who made us and have His power to bring the prodigal home, using the plan our Creator has for marriage.

The skeptic may be saying, "Yes, but you could have put your foot on the brake and stopped her power." No, I don't think I could have done that. We've already established the far country as actually a lonely and miserable place for many prodigals. For over a year, I observed what the world would call an ex-wife (not a very biblical term) who had grown in faithfulness to her God and to her one flesh husband.

If my van were about to go over a cliff and Charlyne knew how to steer it and prevent a disaster, I don't think my foot would have gone for the brake. At some point, your prodigal will have come so close to the cliffs in his far country that he will appreciate a spouse who knows what to do.

Don't be too concerned if your prodigal seems to be operating on smooth ground right now. When he hits the quicksand your efforts will be appreciated. Although there's still a lot about this process I can't understand until I reach eternity, I can testify today that many prodigals come to appreciate and then to embrace their spouses who stand for their marriages. They begin to love them anew. Words escape me to explain the feelings of a prodigal for the standing spouse.

The father placed a ring on his prodigal's hand. Don't be concerned about what has happened to your prodigal's actual wedding ring. You can place an invisible ring on the prodigal's hand by declaring to God your one flesh covenant marriage. Even though a court may have declared a divorce, you can remain married in the eyes of God. The spouse who acknowledges a continuation of that marriage is being obedient to God and His Word.

Most spouses who are standing and praying for their marriages wear their wedding ring on the appropriate finger. Answers to many of life's situations come easily when we consider and declare ourselves married. It's going to be difficult for even the best-intentioned church friend to ask you for a date while you're wearing the ring of your one flesh spouse. Should you be asked out, it's going to be difficult to date wearing that ring. Please check your motives should you ever consider removing your ring for any reason.

Don't be concerned about what others will think or say. You are not denying what has taken place. **You are**

declaring a covenant marriage. While a co-worker may verbalize that you should "take that thing off and have some fun," that person is probably wishing someone had loved them with enough unconditional love to have stood for their own marriage. Most well-intentioned friends won't ask you to do anything contrary to God's Word, but if they ever do, determine ahead of time that you would rather follow God's leading through His Word.

In the parable, the father placed shoes on his prodigal's feet. Perhaps you need to prayerfully place some symbolic shoes on your prodigal's feet. Shoes, even over filthy feet, make walking through life a good bit easier. Shoes make us feel secure, even if we're walking through pig pens. Although not intentional, the spouse at home may have been attempting to make life in the far country uncomfortable for the prodigal. Placing shoes on the prodigal's feet means you desire to make his walk through life a bit more comfortable.

Several years ago while on vacation, I awoke early one morning before the rest of my family. Not wanting to disturb anyone by turning on a light, I attempted to make my way in the dark around our rented efficiency. I walked directly into a table leg, almost breaking a toe. The commotion that ensued woke everyone quicker than if I had turned on a light. Had I been wearing shoes, I still would have run into the table leg, but probably wouldn't have felt the pain or even injured my toes.

Your prodigal is in a strange land, trying to grope his way through the darkness. He's probably running into quite a few table legs and stubbing toes on a regular basis. In some instances, his stubbed toe pain awakens your family. Usually, the prodigal feels the pain alone. The decision to put your symbolic shoes on a prodigal's feet affirms your decision to pray God's best for your spouse, even while he is still groping in the darkness.

One of those old growing-up boyish pranks comes to mind. Someone would tie the shoe laces of an unsuspecting victim together. As soon as he attempted to walk, he would go tumbling, getting a laugh from those involved in the scene. Resist the urge to tie the laces together on your prodigal's shoes. Causing him to fall on his face, emotionally, financially, or in any other way, will not help our God carry out His plan for your marriage. God's timing will be perfect.

The preparation continues. Please don't give up, even for a moment, standing for your marriage. There is coming a day when you will see your prodigal coming back from the far country. No matter how distant, that day will be worth the wait for you, your spouse, your children, your parents, and your friends. Not until eternity will you understand how far-reaching were the effects of your having taken a stand for God's solution to divorce.

PUTTING FAITH INTO ACTION -

We all know families that are separating and facing divorce. Often we respond by listening to part of their story, siding with one of the parties, and then standing by to watch what happens, not really concerned if the marriage ends in divorce. The next time you need encouragement (that's every day for most of us), ask the Lord to direct you to a friend whose marriage seems by the world's standards to be dead and waiting for the funeral. Pray daily for that family. As God directs and gives the opportunity, share the stand you have taken for your marriage. Having to answer some questions about your commitment to marriage will allow you to re-affirm your stand. You'll receive encouragement while you're praying and helping another family say no to divorce. Don't allow Satan to make you believe you don't know enough about standing to help. It's only necessary to be half a step ahead to lead another. I know that by now you are there.

CHAPTER TWELVE

After The Prodigal's Return

"'For this my son was dead and is alive again; he was lost and is found.'" **Luke 15:24 (NKJV)**

Our Lord brings his prodigal children home in many different ways. For some the homecoming is immediate while for others the process is progressive, lasting over an extended period of time. Regardless of how or when your prodigal comes home, there may be several common factors.

You and your spouse both change during the time of separation or divorce. When Charlyne and I were remarried, I thought I knew my wife quite well. After all, we had been married over twenty years before our divorce. Her unconditional love had been evident to me for many months. During the time immediately before our marriage we had experienced an exciting time of dating. By the way, there will come a day when you'll get the flutters when your spouse comes your way, just like in those original dating days. But it wasn't long before I discovered that Charlyne was a totally different person. The things that used to upset her before our divorce now passed without comment. Although far from being a door mat as some separated spouses fear after remarriage, my wife now accepts me as a forgiven person. On the other hand, her loving attitude causes me to want to try harder to please her as my wife. A perpetual motion cycle went into place.

Before our divorce one of my lazy ways was failing to help with household chores without being asked. The nature of my work involves irregular hours, and frequently I'm home in the daytime while my wife is at work.

Previously, I would have to be asked to run the dishwasher. Seldom did I notice the dirty dishes and take care of them on my own. Although these tasks meant little to me, I found they meant a good deal to my wife. Somehow wives use spontaneous help with household chores as a barometer of their husband's love. Taking a few minutes to discover a household chore that needs doing (while she is out of the house) and then carrying out that task pleases my wife. It is unfortunate that a divorce was necessary before I discovered that and about a hundred other little secrets about the woman I love. Please excuse me, I need to start washing a load of towels so they'll be done by 5 P.M.

Perhaps reading through the above paragraphs you've found the real key to happiness after your prodigal returns. No, it isn't Charlyne's changes that are allowing our marriage to be successful; it is the way that Jesus now allows me to look at my wife through different eyes. In summary, our Lord changed me as I watched a wife who was consistently living for Him. I am satisfied settling for second place in her life, because she put Jesus in first place.

It's only fair to tell you that Satan doesn't leave town just because reconciliation is taking place. The one who hates marriage isn't about to allow instant peace and harmony in the home. Yet, there's good news for you. The homecoming that occurred in my life took place after one spouse learned to totally depend on our Lord in every situation. Because of this, there is now power and strength available to us as a reunited couple that can dispel any disruption that Satan tries to again throw in the path of our marriage.

On the day of our remarriage, Charlyne and I made a decision. By that time, we both recognized that Satan is the enemy of marriage, especially in Christian homes. **We made a covenant with one another that, regardless of circumstance, there will never be another separation or divorce in our home. Instead, should problems arise,**

we will take them to God for His solution. We also immediately shared this promise we made to one another with our children.

At some point before the return, your prodigal may approach you, asking you to allow him to store one or a few items in the family's home. The reason may be for safekeeping or so that the children will have them in case anything happens to him. On that day, thank God for the way He is working in your prodigal's life.

Do you recall the mental gathering your prodigal did before he left home? Back then he reasoned that should anything ever happen, he would want to take a particular item with him. On the day your prodigal approaches the family's door with any of his belongings, rejoice that your prodigal has come full cycle. He's now bringing his belongings out of the far country "just in case" anything happens there. Please be confident in God that your prodigal may soon be on the way home to his family.

The actual day of the prodigal's return is a happy but confusing day. The process of rebuilding a family takes time. The spouse at home needs to be most understanding. The far country has been a confusing and lonely place. Don't be alarmed if the homecoming doesn't go quite as smoothly as expected. Please remember that Satan is the author of confusion.

We were married in early July. My employment required that we have a commuting marriage until late September. For over two months, our family continued to be separated by that one hundred miles. The One who knows us best allowed me to gradually return to my home. We would be together each weekend and for one to three other nights during the week. My far country apartment (I finally had one that overlooked a lake) seemed about as appealing as a jail cell when I returned there alone for several days each week.

On the actual day that I was to return home, Satan again tried to discourage our reunion. A change of schedules demanded the rented truck be returned several hours earlier than anticipated. My sons and I started my move home at 4 A.M. By late morning, confusion reigned. The front lawn of our home looked like a dumping site. Some items were to come inside and most of the furniture was being stored in a rented warehouse.

At the time of our remarriage, I had discarded any items that had been gifts or in any way associated with the other person. Nevertheless, on moving day Charlyne questioned where I had obtained a couple of forgotten items. Prodigal, should this happen to you, there is a need for immediate honesty. Your spouse was aware of the other person. Your newly restored marriage deserves to start operating with a policy of complete honesty. Your spouse will appreciate an honest answer from their returned mate.

That night I experienced the best night's sleep that I had known in a long while. There's no feeling like knowing you, your possessions and your family are all safe in the same home. I slept well that night realizing that I was now in obedience to the Lord.

My apartment had been furnished in a style known to many as Early American Divorce. This decor isn't purchased in a store, but is obtained from family hand-me downs, yard sales, and junk piles. Although my old furniture had no value, I didn't want to throw it out. We paid storage for several months. Soon a new family came to our church that had great financial needs. In fact, they needed most of the exact items that we had stored. There was an epilogue to my far country experience when I saw a thankful family sitting on that furniture.

Most prodigals become accustomed to moving. In fact, I moved so often that I had a charge account with a company that makes rubber address stamps. Despite frequent moves, that move home to the family is the most difficult, but the most rewarding. The spouse needs to allow the prodigal to work out his own plans for such matters as combining checking accounts, having mail forwarded, and disposition of duplicate household items.

The couple whose marriage is being restored needs to be especially sensitive to the needs of their children. Please don't become so concerned with each other's needs that the needs of your children are overlooked. Although pleased that there will again be a complete family in their home, your children have seen and heard much since the time of separation. Both parents need to spend time alone with each child as well as spend time together as a family unit.

It was during one of these times alone with my youngest son that he told me, "I'm glad you came home, but I know you won't stay." There was no way I could convince him otherwise, except with time. That thought hasn't been verbalized by my son since those early days.

Prodigal, if your children have become protective of the parent at home, please don't become bitter. Thank God that He used those children to help protect your spouse while you were gone.

Our home has changed a good bit in recent years. Prior to our divorce, the children would seldom have friends over, but things are different now. Our home has become something of a magnet for our children's friends.

It's interesting to notice how many of those friends come from homes with an absent parent or with a step parent. I often suspect our family is being watched carefully by some of our children's friends.

One night recently, wondering how our home could be so noisy, I began reflecting on what all was happening. Tom had his best friend, Jess (from a divorced home) staying over. Lori (able to carry out several tasks at once) was on the phone with a male friend from church. At the same time she was giving some rather straight biblical advice to a girlfriend with a dating problem. Tim was in his room carrying out some project. His southern gospel music was turned up loud enough that we could all enjoy it with him. Charlyne was writing out a couple of cards of encouragement for women she was working with in her Sunday School class.

There is no pleasure the far country could offer that compared with my joy as I realized why our home was noisy. Perhaps with spiritual eyes, another prodigal can see his restored family ministering to other hurting people.

One final red flag. The restored couple needs to be extremely careful in financial matters. There will again be two incomes and only one set of household expenses. On the other hand, one or both spouses may have borrowed money or used credit cards while living apart. Some couples tend to do some careless spending and celebrating after the prodigal returns.

There are several helps available to the Christian family desiring to establish a budget. We want to give you the most important advice even before the budget book is opened. Give God His tithe regardless of the circumstances. God will always meet your need if you are faithful in your tithe. The Bible says, *"He will rebuke the devourer, for your sake." **Malachi 3:11***

Our Lord may bring your prodigal home under completely different circumstances. When a spouse is praying for the marriage to be restored, **unconditional love says that the prodigal is already forgiven and will be accepted home at any time and in any condition.**

Should bankruptcy or serious illness make it necessary for the prodigal to return home, our Jesus knows the purpose even for that problem. Consider my friend who answered her phone one afternoon. The caller introduced herself as the husband's girlfriend. She stated that he had been taken to the doctor, was seriously ill, and needed to be admitted to the hospital for surgery. She announced that the ill man and his luggage in her car were being returned home. It seems other persons don't hold up well when the road of life becomes rough. Although under unusual circumstances, another prodigal had come home.

A common question deals with the need for counseling when a spouse is returning. As with other matters, let God direct you and your spouse as individuals, as He reveals the needs of your family. Please don't consider seeking counseling as a weakness. Much has probably taken place in the lives of all concerned that could use some release. Should you seek counsel, look only to the individual who uses the Bible as his guide. Your pastor might be a wise place to start.

Although I won't give any advice regarding counseling, I will advise you about The Counselor. It is critical that you and your spouse, as soon as your prodigal is back home, develop a daily devotional time together. Our God desires for the restored couple to totally depend on Him for every need and every problem.

What is the greatest day for the returning prodigal? I don't know. We have been remarried for many years. There are still some ups and downs, but every day gets better and better. Perhaps other books need to be written later to tell you how great marriage can be after the prodigal returns.

PUTTING FAITH INTO ACTION -

One of the most overlooked words in the Bible is that little word fasting. We're beginning to understand prayer, but fasting is still a foreign topic to many. Consider doing some self-study on the topic of biblical fasting. The results of fasting will be an encouragement to you.

Epilogue

Last evening our family attended the first night of revival services at our church. We sat with one of the young women from Charlyne's Sunday School class. Karen's husband left their home a few months ago. Property settlement papers are being signed this week. Unless God intervenes, she soon will be divorced. Her problems associated with the divorce are many. Despite all, Karen is standing for her marriage.

After having worked a long day, Karen arranged for a relative to babysit so that she could be present for that service. As we stood to sing, two things could be noticed about her. She was holding a hymnal in her left hand, and on her finger were her wedding rings. On her youthful face was that smile that only total fellowship with Jesus Christ can bring.

Although unknown to those involved, many other couples are watching all the Karen's in our church. At times the message from the pew seems louder than the message from the pulpit. Their lives are proclaiming: *When your marriage falls apart, find an altar, not an attorney.*

Thank you for allowing us to share our story with you. Our prayer is that the Lord may take each illustration and give it His application for your life.

May our Mighty God bless you, encourage you, and support you as you seek His will for your family.

Bob and Charlyne Steinkamp

Charlyne's Prayer For Families

Today pray for the many families struggling with severe marriage problems at home and pray for each family that has a prodigal in the far country. Let's pray:

Lord, we come together in agreement where in Matthew 18:19 we read that if two of you on earth agree about anything we ask for, it will be done for us by our Father in Heaven. For where two or three come together in My name, there am I with them. Lord, we pray that no weapon formed against this family will prevail. Satan, you were defeated at the cross when our Lord Jesus Christ was crucified. He arose showing you His mighty power. Get away from this family and all families around the world who are speaking separation and divorce. God hates divorce, instead He will be the Repairer of Broken Walls, a Repairer of the Breech and will rebuild homes on the solid rock of Jesus Christ.

Lord, we are praying that this couple and all our prodigals around the world will have a personal relationship with You as their Savior and as their Lord. For it is by grace that each of us has been saved through faith, not of ourselves, but a gift from God. Lord, we are putting the full Armor of God on this family and on all the families around the world who have strife of separation going on in their homes, putting a hedge of protection and the blood of Jesus over them, so that we can take a stand against the devil's schemes. We stand in agreement with our Lord God and know that all of the enemy's tricks and schemes against this family and other families are broken.

For our struggles are not against flesh and blood, but against the rulers, against the authorities, against the powers of this dark world and against the spiritual forces of evil in the heavenly realms. Lord, we pray that all the spouses who are planning on leaving and the ones who are gone will flee the evil desires of youth, and instead pursue righteousness, faith, love and peace, along with those who call on the Lord out of a pure heart. We pray that they will come to their senses and escape from the trap of the devil, who has taken them captive to do his will. We know that Your sheep hear Your voice, so speak loudly to Your children today and we pray that they will be obedient to Your voice, Your will and Your way.

Lord, we praise You that You are in control of this crisis. We pray that You will show Your people the power of prayer. Give hope to husbands and wives, showing them and speaking to them that You can heal, restore and rebuild their marriage. Nothing is too hard for You, and greater is He that is in us than he who is in the world.

Lord, we praise You and thank You that we have confidence in approaching You; that if we ask anything according to Your will, You hear us. And we know that when You hear us – whatever we ask – we know that we have what we asked of You. We pray 1 Corinthians 13:4-8 on them, restoring their love as the day each of them got married. Lord, we give this couple and all other couples around the world to You Lord, and trust You to protect them from the evil one. We pray this in the mighty name of our Lord Jesus Christ. Amen.

MEET THE STEINKAMPS

Bob and Charlyne's marriage was not always blissful. They separated several times and finally divorced in 1986 after 20 years of marriage and with three children.

Charlyne searched the Scriptures and discovered that God hates divorce. She found that our Lord Jesus Christ restores and rebuilds marriages when a mate will love the prodigal unconditionally, as Christ loves us. Charlyne committed herself to a sacrificial stand for the restoration of their marriage. To the glory of God, Bob and Charlyne were remarried on July 7, 1987.

God allowed Bob and Charlyne to minister His love, forgiveness and restoration to others with broken marriages for over twenty years. In December 2010, Bob lost his battle with cancer and end-stage heart disease. Today, Charlyne and her family continue to proclaim the message that *God Heals Hurting Families.*

You may be reading this book searching for someone to help your marriage problems. His name is Jesus. Please contact us if Rejoice Marriage Ministries can help you discover the difference that the Lord can make in your hurting or dead marriage.

*But blessed is the man who trusts in the Lord, whose confidence is in Him. **Jeremiah 17:7***

THE GREATEST NEWS

That if you confess with your mouth, "Jesus is Lord," and believe in your heart that God raised him from the dead, you will be saved. **Romans 10:9**

Have you received Jesus Christ as Lord and Savior of your life? He will save you and be your Comforter and Counselor in the days ahead, regardless of the circumstances. Many people in a hurting marriage have discovered that the first step in a healed marriage is to have a personal relationship with Jesus Christ. Our God and Creator is waiting to hear your prayer.

A Prayer For You

"Dear Jesus, I believe that You died for me and that You rose again on the third day. I confess to You that I am a sinner and that I need Your love and forgiveness. Come into my life, forgive me of my sins, and give me eternal life. I confess to You now that You are my Lord and Savior. Thank You for my salvation. Lord, show me Your will and Your way for my marriage. Mold me and make me to be the spouse I need to be for my mate. Thank You for rebuilding my marriage. *Amen.*"

Signed_____

Date_____

"...Believe in the Lord Jesus, and you will be saved -- you and your household." **Acts 16:31**

TEN SOURCES OF HELP

Here are ten ways that Rejoice Marriage Ministries, Inc. can help you stay encouraged as you stand strong with God and pray for the restoration of your family.

Prayer – The number one source of help for your marriage is centered on prayer. While we have several prayer lists and an online Chapel, our goal is to teach you how to pray for your prodigal, for yourself, and for your loved ones.

The Bible – We strive to teach you how to get your answers from the Word of God. "Someone said," really should not carry much weight with what you do. Instead, read God's Word daily, seeking His will for your life and marriage. God does speak to His children.

Web Site – The Rejoice Marriage Ministries Web site has over a thousand pages of helps, including Q & A, praise reports from standers, testimonies from restored marriages, audio teleconference recordings and much more to help you be able to stand for healing of your marriage. http://RejoiceMinistries.org

Charlyne Cares – Seven days a week we send subscribers a daily devotional by that name. Always based on Scripture, Charlyne teaches on topics that will help you grow in the Lord as you pray for your marriage. We also offer a men's and kid's devotional that is sent weekly. Subscribe for free from http://charlyne.org/

Stop Divorce Radio – We broadcast good music and Good News around the clock for men and women facing marriage problems. You will hear Charlyne and men of God teaching on marriage restoration. You can listen while you work or play. http://StopDivorceRadio.org

God Heals Hurting Marriages – Our five-minute weekday audio program. We encourage you to get into the habit of listening every day. You will be amazed how often the program's subject will be exactly what you need to hear for that day to be encouraged in the Lord. http://rejoiceministries.org/radio.html

Fight For Your Marriage – A weekly 30-minute audio Bible study online, during which Charlyne teaches you God's Word on how to grow in the Lord, pray for your family and fight for the healing and restoration of your marriage. http://rejoiceministries.org/radio.html

Stop Divorce Bookstore – Our online bookstore offers marriage restoration teaching in books and on CDs. We also have other items available, such as front license plates, bracelets and Spanish material. http://StopDivorce.org

Rejoice Pompano – Standers in South Florida meet with us here in Pompano Beach each month for Bible study, worship, prayer, support and fellowship. From time to time we also take *Rejoice on the Road* to other communities. http://RejoicePompano.org

Personal Contact – Our goal is for you to develop a personal relationship with Jesus Christ. When He is Savior and Lord of your life, you can allow Him to direct every step in your life and marriage.

We have many other helps available for the man or woman who is seeking marriage restoration God's way. We encourage you to take advantage of the other resources available by visiting our web site.

For nothing is impossible with God. **Luke 1:37**

Rejoice Marriage Ministries, Inc.
www.rejoiceministries.org